D0292338

JERICHO

JERICHO

A NOVEL BY

Janet Hickman

Greenwillow Books

N E W YORK

EVERMAN PUBLIC LIBRARY

OCT 9 6   11,983

Copyright © 1994 by Janet Hickman
All rights reserved. No part of this book may be reproduced
or utilized in any form or by any means, electronic or
mechanical, including photocopying, recording,
or by any information storage and retrieval system, without
permission in writing from the Publisher, Greenwillow Books,
a division of William Morrow & Company, Inc.,
1350 Avenue of the Americas, New York, NY 10019.
Printed in the United States of America
First Edition   10 9 8 7 6 5

Library of Congress Cataloging-in-Publication Data
Hickman, Janet.
Jericho / by Janet Hickman.
p.   cm.
Summary: An account of twelve-year-old Angela's visit
to help take care of her great-grandmother alternates
with the story of the old woman's life.
ISBN 0-688-13398-3
[1. Great-grandmothers—Fiction.
2. Family life—Fiction.]
I. Title.   PZ7.J5314Je   1994
[Fic]—dc20   93-37309   CIP   AC

FOR MY MOTHER

JERICHO

1

ANGELA'S GREAT-GRANDMOTHER stares at her with faded, puzzled eyes that make the girl long to be home. They are a stranger's eyes in a color-less face, studying her as if she is a brand new item, an alien.

"Are you all right, GrandMin?" Angela asks. She is trying to do what her mother and Gram want—keep GrandMin occupied, give them a minute's peace.

The great-grandmother only frowns and ad-justs the sharp angles of her shoulders against the backrest of her wheelchair. People's bones shouldn't stick out like that, Angela thinks, and looks away. She has seen old pictures of GrandMin when she was different, a plump woman shapeless in the middle, with birdlike ankles. Now her remaining weight has shifted downward like rotting potatoes slumped in the bottom of a bag.

Suddenly the old woman inclines her body forward, toward the window. "What are they doing to my house?" She points with her whole hand.

"Painting it." Angela takes a magazine from the table by Gram's sofa and sits down. That is nine times today for the same question. How does Gram stand taking care of her all the time, listening and answering, listening and answering? The clock on the desk chimes twice. Oh, to be home, Angela thinks, to have cable TV, the library two blocks away, and the pool where she goes sometimes on days like this in spite of the way her swimsuit fits. She wants to be with Tessa. Need for her best friend, for someone young and funny, comes up into her throat. In all of this tiny town where her mother's family lives, there is not one girl her age. Not one.

Dear Tessa, she composes in her head. *This is much worse than even I expected. Imagine nothing to do, subtract two, and that's my summer so far. Keeping an eye on my great-grandmother doesn't count. Neither does helping my dad scrape wallpaper. Some great idea my parents had for a vacation.*

"What did you say they were doing to my house?" Min's gaze travels again across the neat wide lawn outside the window and on to the next lot. "There's a bunch of people around the back," she says. "I see them every once in a while. You don't suppose they're trying to break in?"

"No, GrandMin, they're painting," Angela says. Ten times now for that question. She is careful not to say, "They're fixing it up to rent it maybe." That is the truth, but it is the wrong thing to say; she tried it yesterday. "They're making it look really nice, don't you think? The way it used to be, I bet. Want me to wheel you out on the porch so you can see?"

"No," Min says slowly. "Katy doesn't like it if I go away."

"You know Gram won't care if you just go out on the porch." Angela gets up to find her sandals.

"No," Min says again. She loses focus, blinks, looks at the girl. "Who did you say you were?"

Angela takes a breath. She hates this part. As often as the question comes, she can't get used to it. "I'm Angela," she says, shaking out the lengths of crinkled copper-brown hair that most people remember her by. "You know—I'm Carol's daughter. Carol, your granddaughter. So I'm your great-granddaughter. You know me, GrandMin. You've been seeing me off and on ever since I was a baby." Over twelve years, thinks Angela, and shivers without meaning to. There is something about being unrecognized, unnamed, that bothers her beyond words.

Min is shaking her head. "No," she says, "Carol had a boy. He was a cute little thing, too."

"That's Brian," Angela says, resentment edging into her voice. "He's my brother. He's only two years older than I am, GrandMin. Why can't you remember me, too?"

Min considers for a moment, then tilts one shoulder in a shrug. "Whoever you are," she says, "you have pretty hair." Angela blinks back the sudden prickles behind her eyelids and turns away for a moment, embarrassed that she can still be hurt by something that happens so often. Min takes no notice. She gives her attention to the window and forgets Angela all over again.

"You know," the old woman says in a new tone, "there's a mystery here. I don't know what they've done with Jericho."

Angela clears her throat. "It's okay, GrandMin. This *is* Jericho. I mean, it may be Gatesville now, but it's the same place. It's just that nobody has called it Jericho since you were young. That's what my mom says."

Min's old eyes do not flicker. She stares through the window toward her old house with new paint, the highway, and beyond to the frame church half hidden by maple trees, other houses, a tiny post office, a store. "No one knows what they've done with it," she says.

Talking to my great-grandmother is just like watch-

ing one of those old Twilight Zone reruns on cable, Angela adds to Tessa's letter in her head. Aloud she says, "Where do you think you are, GrandMin?"

Min begins to fuss with the handkerchief on the front of her dress. It is pinned there to keep her from losing track of it. "Well," she whispers, "they *say* this is Jericho. They tell me it is."

Angela bites her lower lip as if that can keep Min's from trembling. "It's okay, Gran," she says, feeling a sudden pain for Min that is almost as great as the one she carries for her own bored and lonely self. She pats the little hump on her great-grandmother's back, touching carefully, almost fearfully. "I'm sorry," she says. "It isn't the same as it used to be, is it?"

"If I could just go home," Min says to the window. "But they tell me the folks are all gone. Pa and everyone. Kate tells me there's no one left."

Angela shudders. "Ring the bell here on your tray if you need anything. Okay, GrandMin? I have to go do something." What she has to do is go cry in private. It is more than she can bear to think of all Min's people dead, all their lives behind them, and Min still yearning after them.

In the bathroom Angela uses up the last of Gram's scented tissues because GrandMin cannot possibly go home the way she wants to, although she, Angela, could be home right now. There is hand cream beside the sink, and it makes her think of Tessa, who has an astonishing collection of perfumes and lotions and makeup. Whenever she or Angela feels downhearted, Tessa hurries to apply some new combination of eyeliners or outrageous nail colors. Angela always takes hers off before she goes home, but it helps anyway. In Gram's cupboard there is not so much as one bottle of clear polish, nor any other remedy for whatever it is that makes her feel the way she does. The family visit to Gram's, two more empty weeks of it, lies waiting.

By suppertime Angela is composed. She has volunteered for chores that separate her from Min and her questions. She has even found time to read a magazine story and announce how sad it was to ward off remarks about the lingering redness of her eyes. Now the family gathers close in the grandparents' kitchen, hot as it is, around the knobby-legged table. Gram and Grandpa have the ends of the table and the chairs with cushions. Between them on one side are Angela's parents, smelling faintly of turpentine. She sits on the other side with Brian. All accounted for again. The routine of regular mealtimes seemed cozy at first, but now she misses the easier pace of eating at home, even though

Gram's cooking is far superior to anything she has ever found in a microwave tray.

Brian tries to be funny, as usual. When the three-bean casserole comes around, he says, "I don't do vegetables," and everyone laughs except Angela. She has heard all her life that girls adore their older brothers, but she has never thought of Brian that way. It annoys her that it is so easy for him to charm other people by clowning around. She almost never laughs at him, and he almost always teases her anyway.

"Hey, Angie—" Whatever he is saying to her now gets lost in the sound of GrandMin's bell, which rings with increasing insistence from the living room where, by her own request, she sits alone with her meal. Angela stands up. She is remembering that her father has offered to give her extra spending money for helping out here, to make up for what she could have earned baby-sitting at home.

"I'll go see if she's finished with her tray, Gram."

"No, Angela," Gram says. "It's me she wants."

"Katy?" Min is calling. "Katy?" There is an edge of panic in her voice.

"Right here, Min. I'm coming." Gram gets up and Angela eases back into her chair, thinking how tired her grandmother sounds. Gram is always answering Min and going to her, over and over. GrandMin seldom remembers where she is. Once, Angela knows, Gram bought a child's slate for messages—I am doing the laundry, I am walking out to the road to bring in the paper, I am cleaning the bedrooms upstairs—and put it beside Min in the wheelchair. But then Min forgot to look at it and called anyway: "Kate? Katy? Where did you go?"

Now Kate hurries to her mother's call, and in spite of herself Angela strains to hear their voices over the family chatter at the table.

"Do you have to go right this minute, Min? Can it wait a little bit?"

"No, I did it already. I didn't mean to. I couldn't tell."

"Well, my . . . We'll take care of it. You've only got one clean shift left, I think. If only you would ring a little sooner."

"I couldn't tell, Katy. I just didn't know. You know I'm no use to anybody. I just pray to die, but the good Lord won't have me. You might as well take a gun and shoot me, and then you wouldn't have all this fuss."

"Stop it, Min. Don't talk like that." Gram's voice comes suddenly loud. "Angel? Would you be a good girl and dish up the dessert for everyone, please? Your mom's too tired, and I'm going to be awhile in the bathroom with GrandMin."

"Sure, Gram." Angela finds a smile for Brian. "You don't do dessert either, do you?" She clenches her teeth for the poke under the table that is sure to come, but even this diversion doesn't shut out the thought that right now Gram is cleaning GrandMin like a big old baby.

———

Arminda was the smallest, and no one would listen to her. Lucy was seven already, more than two years older. And Delia was fourteen. Delia was beautiful, too, with a wonderful mouth that turned up at the corners even when she wasn't smiling.

When Arminda tried to speak, Delia's lips went right on moving, chiding the brothers, begging Pa to eat.

"It's good, isn't it?" Delia insisted. "I used the new potatoes."

"Fine," Jesse said. He was the oldest brother, taller than Pa.

William was second oldest, the one who was always right. He was louder than Pa, but he didn't say anything about the food.

"Tastes like hog slop to me," said Wheat, whose real name was Jacob. He was not much older than Delia, and he was a trial to her.

"Please," whispered Arminda, "I have to—"

"Eat, Pa." Delia finished frowning at Wheat

and let her lips fall into a pout. "We don't want you to be weak and sickly now. And I'm not such a bad cook, am I? You'll make the boys think I'm a bad cook."

Sam Walters gave his head a shake that made his droopy mustache wiggle. "I don't feel too hungry tonight, girl," he said. "I've a mind to walk over to the cemetery."

Arminda wiggled. "Can I go to the—"

Lucy kicked her under the table, button shoe to button shoe, and giggled. Lucy was a giggler. "Bedtime for babies, Min," she whispered. "You can't go anywhere."

"Oh, Pa, do you have to?" Delia wrinkled her smooth face. "Take some flowers then. I'll cut you some snowballs off the bush. Wait till I find the shears."

Arminda began to feel her own dampness against the seat of her chair. She cried.

"Where are those shears?" Delia was banging around in the sewing cupboard. "Were you little girls playing with the shears? Is that it?" Delia's eyes twinkled like little biting teeth when she scolded.

"Not me!" sang Lucy. "I never saw the shears."

"Mercy!" Delia turned to the smallest one. "Look at the guilty one cry. What makes you so naughty? Our Mama not gone a week and you snitching things already."

"I didn't! I didn't!" screamed Arminda. "They're in the big box with Mama, right down by the cushion. I saw. Aunt Abel cut a piece off the end of the flower in there and then she put the shears down and I was afraid to reach in, and that's where they are. They're with my mama!"

Her father groaned. "Oh, dear God," he said, "we've buried the shears with Molly."

Arminda stopped her tears. Someone had listened to her. She was pleased. When she went to bed she took care of her own wet skirt, hanging the dress to dry over the windowsill before Lucy had a chance to see it.

2

THE SECOND WEEK of Angela's visit is bearable because she discovers a hoard of books that had been her mother's. Gram sends her to the attic for canning jars, and there beside them, like a gift, are dusty cartons with faded labels and plenty to read. Her mother has already tried to get books for her at the library in New Liberty, twenty miles away, but guest cards allow only three books at a time. Angela reads like fire in dry grass; three books make no more than a spark. Now she is happy for two whole days, reading what her mother once read, feeling that she has a new, secret bond with the rumpled woman in the paint-smeared slacks. She does not offer to talk about the stories with her mother because Carol is a teacher and asks too many questions, offers too many explanations. "Will there be a quiz?" Brian often says to his mother in a mocking tone, and then even Angela thinks he is funny.

What is best about the books is that they transport her above the tick-tock repetition of GrandMin's routines. She holds *Rebecca* open against her hip when she is roused out of it to fetch and carry for her great-grandmother. "Here's your pill, GrandMin," she says, or, "Let me take your tray, okay?" But seldom do the old woman's eyes trap her and remind her she is stranded without friends on an island of oldness, still days away from rescue.

As the week wears on, Angela's parents begin to exchange looks over her head. "Don't bring that book to the table," her father warns gently at Wednesday lunchtime. It signals one of many issues brought from home to Gatesville unnoticed, like socks in the corner of a suitcase: Angela reads too much, Brian reads too little; Brian never meets a stranger, Angela never makes a friend; Brian is overscheduled, Angela doesn't get enough activity; Angela doesn't talk enough, Brian talks too much. Balance, balance. She slips her paper napkin in the book to mark the page and sighs.

"Don't want to ruin your eyes, Angel," says her grandfather, who has taken the week off from work to help with GrandMin's house. His voice is so kind and apologetic—*he* wouldn't care if she read at the table—that she wants to climb up in his lap and eat from his plate. She did that once as a tiny girl, curling her lips around one single baked bean after another speared on the tip of Grandpa's fork. "Look at me feed this sparrow, will you?" the memory says.

Carol speaks briskly. "Angie, maybe you'd like to do something better than hang around the house this afternoon. Maybe you could help us over at Min's." She looks at her husband, who is making a face. "Now, Jay, she can't learn to do things like painting if we don't give her a chance."

"I'd really rather finish the book," Angela says, eyes on her plate. "And help with GrandMin, of course."

She feels rather than sees the look that passes between her mother and Gram. Then it is Gram's voice, irresistible as always, because Angela so loves her grandmother.

"You know what I'd like someone to do? I've been meaning to take a few flowers up to the cemetery for Grandpa Walters's grave, but I'm just too tired to trek up that hill. He had a June birthday, and I always try to put something out for him."

Brian helps himself to a third sandwich. "Angie can take it up," he says. "The exercise will do her good. She's getting to be a real buffalo butt."

Carol and Gram say "Brian!" in unison. Angela wants to disappear. She wants to hurt Brian and then disappear. He has no room to talk about her size, him with his own big square chunky frame. Still, she hates, *hates*, to be reminded of her own body, which isn't yet right, too big here, too small there, an affront to every mirror. Silently she promises herself revenge. To Gram she says, "I'll go whenever you want."

When the meal is over and the dishes are dried, when GrandMin is put to bed for a sleepless rest, then Gram cuts sweet william and bachelor's buttons and a few roses from her fence-row garden. She arranges them in one of the canning jars that Angela brought from the attic. "Be careful on the highway, Angel," she says. "The cars come over that hill so fast."

"Okay, Gram," says Angela, as if her journey might actually be dangerous rather than mostly in sight of the house. "I'll be careful."

It is uncomfortably hot as she follows the edge of the road, plodding upward. The cemetery is not a place she wants to visit, with or without flowers. By the time she goes between the gray stone pillars that mark the entrance, her hands ache from stretching around the jar. Angela tries to concentrate on remembering directions: follow the driveway to the right, pass one path, start looking for the Walters memorial stone on the left. She knows that everything living has to die, but it is troubling to think of real people—family people—resting here, under this ground. Resting is such a funny word for it, she thinks, and wishes hard for home. She never thinks of things like this at home. *Save me, Tessa,* she writes in her mind. Tessa watches Stephen King movies without flinching. *Maybe your parents would let you come visit me here.* She knows that is hopeless, but she thinks about it anyway and fails to see a garden rake on the gravel in front of her.

"Watch out!" cries a voice so unexpected that Angela's muscles jerk to a stop before she has time to be afraid. Water sloshes out of the flower jar, making her pink T-shirt cling awkwardly to her stomach.

"Hi," the voice says. "What are you looking for?" At last Angela sees the speaker, a boy near Brian's age, maybe younger. He crouches in jeans and no shirt beside a tall tombstone, clipping the grass around its base.

"Wish I had a Weed Eater," he says to her silence. His hair is pale and straight. "You trying to find somebody special?"

Her tongue sticks to her teeth. She doesn't know this person. She checks her mental list of Gatesville people that her mother and grandparents talk about and still has no idea who he could be.

"Walters," she says finally, feeling utterly stupid. "My grandmother said to bring these."

He rocks back on his heels and considers her with the kind of curious look that boys sometimes give Tessa, eyes sweeping downward and flicking back up to rest on her face or her hair, she can't tell which. Instinctively she holds the flowers tight against her middle. She knows she is blushing.

"The Walters stone is right about there," he says, pointing. He has a very serious expression. "You visiting or what?"

"Just visiting."

"Staying long?"

"No." She mumbles her thanks for the directions and hurries on around the curving driveway, avoiding the rake, pretending not to hear that he calls after her to ask her name. She doesn't even stop to read the inscription on the Walters stone, just plops down the flowers and then circles the whole cemetery to avoid seeing the boy on the way out.

Going back to Gram's, something prompts her to run. The afternoon heat is rising, but she has energy. Maybe it is all the walking, she thinks, but she hates for her parents to be right about exercise. When she slows down for the porch steps, her breath comes with a rasping sound.

Brian is waiting for her at the screen. "Alert!" he calls. "Buffalo stampede! Sounds like one is wounded!"

"Idiot," Angela says, panting. "You'll wake up GrandMin."

"Too late. She's already awake. Gram says go see what she wants. I have to go help Dad."

Angela wipes her damp face on the hem of her shirt and goes reluctantly into Min's bedroom. It closes her in with its clean, terrible smells: liniment, disinfectant, dusting powder.

"Do you need something, GrandMin?" she asks. The old woman lies silent, watching.

"GrandMin?" Angela waits a moment, then turns to leave.

"Don't go," whispers the face in the bed. "The others have all gone and left me."

Angela sits on the edge of the chair nearest the door. "Okay. We can talk, I guess. Why don't you tell me about Jericho?" She is proud of herself for thinking of this, but she hopes Gram will come soon. "Tell me about when you were little," she says to GrandMin.

Min turns her head toward the girl. "Oh, I can't do that," she says. "That was years and years ago. I can't remember."

———

The grass in the field was high and sweet, the sky above it huge and smooth as a giant blue crock overturned. Important clouds edged along the horizon, changing their colors in the evening's last sun. Lucy tugged Arminda farther from the house.

"Here," she said, "here's a good place." She flopped full-length, pulling her sister down beside her. "Look up, baby Min. Do you see it?"

"I'm not a baby." Min snatched her hand away from Lucy's and tried to ignore the sky. She didn't have to look at it if she didn't want to. Lucy couldn't make her. But oh, it was beautiful. Through the slits of her half-closed eyes she saw puffs of rose and gold and cream above the hill where the cemetery was, towers in the sky, shifting.

"Look," Lucy whispered in her dreaming voice. "That's heaven. That's where our mama is. Up there with all the pretty colors. Don't it look soft, Min? Better than a feather tick."

The cemetery hill humped in dark outline against the colors of the sky, its headstones jutting up like old blunt thorns. Min felt trouble settle over her. How could Mama be up in the sky on a feather tick when Pa went to the hill every night to sit beside her?

"Look over that way," Lucy said. "The little puff off by itself—that's an angel, I bet." Her finger pointed and Min's eyes followed. They were pale eyes that changed from gray to green to steely blue, not soft blue and transparent like Lucy's. Lucy's eyes saw things that never were.

"Is it an angel for real and true?" Min asked, wanting it to be. Delia sang a song about angels sometimes; angels were nice.

"Hello, little girls." A voice came suddenly above them, out of sight behind their heads.

Min's heart thumped as she whirled onto her stomach and stared up at an old face, bearded and stern. Maybe it was God, she thought, and he had heard them talking and wanted to make sure they had it right. He seemed friendly enough.

"What are you doing out here all by yourselves?"

Min smiled up at him. His head looked very far away, like God, but he wore regular brown leather shoes, like Pa. "We're looking at an angel," she said.

"Shh," hissed Lucy, whose pale cheeks had turned to ghost flesh in the fading light. "She's just a baby, Mr. Bagley."

"I am not," said Arminda, considering whether Lucy could be wrong about this being Mr. Bagley.

"I know she is," said Mr. Bagley–God, "and a very pretty baby she is, too. I want to have a word with your father, little ones. Could you tell me where he might be?"

"He's up on the hill with our mama," Arminda said quickly, in the voice that Delia always said was too sassy.

"No, sir!" Lucy corrected. "He went home." She frowned at her little sister.

A shadow passed over Mr. Bagley's face as he touched his hand to his straw hat and walked away. The two girls lay silent for a time, watching the clouds and each other.

"I should be the one to talk to people," Lucy announced finally. "I'm the oldest."

"I can talk if I want to," Min told her.

"You're a bad baby," Lucy said soberly.

"Am not." Min's insides began to quiver.

"Yes, you are," Lucy insisted. "Delia says so. You're a bad baby because you sass back. Delia *hates* when you sass back."

Min's eyes were drowning. "No, sir," she said. "Delia likes me." Min thought of Delia's soft lap, the only one in the house. "She likes me, Lucy." But panic came over Min—what if Delia didn't like her?—and she stumbled to her feet. She ran blindly toward the house, dripping tears and hoping for Delia to find her and hug her. Maybe she would give Lucy a switching for being so mean.

When she came near the porch she saw with

relief that Delia was there. But she wasn't alone. Pa was with her, and so was Mr. Bagley. Min turned shy and ducked beneath the snowball bush that grew at the corner of the porch. Generous leaves covered her with a patchwork of green-silver, long soft stems trapped her between the smell of earth and the cool touch of the house's stone foundation. It was one of Min's favorite places, otherworldly and comforting. She wiped her nose on the hem of her dress, and when her own breathing was no longer loud in her ears, she listened to the voices.

"Mrs. Bagley and I," said the visitor, "well, we have chewed this over for many an hour, Sam. You know how she's grieving for your Molly. We both are. And it's only us thinking how Molly would want her baby looked after that makes us offer. Your Delia here is a peach, make no mistake about that. But how's she ever going to be able to cook and wash and clean for all your big fellows and then look after two little ones besides?" He cleared his throat. "Now, Lucy's got enough age to her to help out some, but that littlest one is going to be a lot of care here, where she'd be nothing but a blessing to us. We'd take her right in like our own and keep her as long as you'd want. Mother always did set great store by a little girl."

Sam Walters's wooden rocker rumbled against

the porch floor. It was loud in Min's ear, and she could feel it, too, vibrating at the edge of the nearest board. *Scree-chunk, scree-chunk, scree-chunk,* through a long, long time with no talking.

"Much obliged to you, Bagley," her pa said at last, "but I don't know how I could give her up."

The words stirred in Arminda's head. Give who up? What did he mean?

"Maybe you should think on it, Sam," the other man said.

The rocking stopped. "God, Bagley, that's just too hard. You got to remember that little Min is my baby, too, just as much as Molly's."

Little Min. *Baby.* The word smarted like red pepper on a sore lip. The baby opened her mouth to protest.

But it was Delia whose voice broke in on the men. "Pa! Don't you dare let anyone take Arminda! I won't let you, I swear it!" The words rose out of control. "No one else can have her!"

Then Min herself rose up out of the snowball bush, wailing. "You can't have me!" she shouted. "You can't have me!" She scrambled onto the porch and flung herself into Delia's lap, terrified and triumphant. Delia loves me, Lucy, she thought. So there.

3

ON FRIDAY MORNING Angela goes to New Liberty with her mother. It is mostly a grocery trip, which is boring, but there is time for the mall. She has been there on other visits to Gram's and knows that the shops have little to offer. Even so, she is grateful for the sight of new faces. She notices hairstyles and decides that New Liberty girls must watch the same TV shows as her friends at home.

Carol says she will buy Angela a pair of running shorts, and Angela agrees because they are turquoise. She does not intend to run in them.

"Tessa has a pair just like these, I think," she says.

Her mother gives her a quick one-armed hug right there at the checkout counter. "I know you miss her," Carol says. "It won't be much longer now. There are days I think we can never finish that house, but honestly, Angie, I promise there will be an end to it."

Angela is afraid that other shoppers are staring at them. "I love Gram and Grandpa," she says softly, edging away from her mother. "That's not it." She doesn't know what to say about Min. "I'd just rather be home, you know?"

"I know. We all have reasons for wanting to be home." Carol pushes back some hair that has fallen across her forehead, and Angela is surprised to notice silver glints that couldn't be paint. "We have reasons for wanting to be with Gram, too," Carol says. "That's what makes it so hard. Min is just wearing Mother out."

She wears us all out, Angela thinks, but she doesn't want to say it. She would rather talk about Tessa and running shorts than about the Min problem. There has been endless discussion about it already during this vacation—how to help Gram, how to deal with Min's house, how to provide for Min now that she has slipped so far but seems so strong. Angela feels it has nothing to do with her, nothing and yet somehow everything. It is confusing and sad.

Her mother hands over the package and wants to hurry. "I have one more little stop," she says, heading for the parking lot. "It's just to satisfy my own curiosity, and you can stay in the car and listen to the radio if you'd rather."

"No, I'll come," Angela says, without knowing where. Her mother drives to a low brick building with a sign that says ValleyCare Nursing Center. Angela almost changes her mind. GrandMin times ten, she thinks, and then suspicion overtakes her. "What are you going to do?"

"Just checking," Carol says as they get out of the car. "I want to find out what their rates are like, see what the place looks like inside."

"Does Gram know you're here?"

Carol shakes her head. "I worry about what would happen if Min gets worse or if something happens to Mom. We have to think about alternatives, that's all."

While her mother goes to find the office, Angela sits in the waiting room, trying not to think about alternatives. The floor is glaringly clean. Everything smells like GrandMin's bedroom, plus extra antiseptic and vegetable soup. It is early, but it seems to be lunchtime. She can bend forward and see people in another room around a table. Some are in chairs, some in wheelchairs, not talking much, waiting. Someone begins to wail, "Ohhh, David, David, David. Oh, David!" Another voice comes soothing, shushing. Angela shivers. Who is David? Then women in pink uniforms begin to bring the meals, and their voices are loud and cheerful. Angela hopes her mother will hurry.

She picks up a magazine and moves to another

chair, one facing away from the dining room. In this new seat Angela has a clear view into a room in which a very old woman sits alone. She is bound into her wheelchair with a strip of sheeting that runs across her chest and under her arms. Her body cannot slump, but her head rolls from side to side on a neck as limp as the stem of an unwatered plant.

"Lunchtime, Gracie!" calls one of the pink women. She comes carrying a bowl and a long plastic tube with a squeeze bulb on one end. Gram has one of these, Angela realizes; she uses it for basting the Thanksgiving turkey. "Open wide, Gracie!" the attendant says.

Angela feels as if all her insides are shifting. GrandMin should never come here, she thinks. She goes outside to wait near the entrance until her mother is finished, and on the way home she barely listens as Carol recites prices in a dull voice. "We won't say anything about this to your Gram," Carol says, and Angela nods. It is not something she wants to talk about at all.

"Let's see the new shorts," her mother says when they are back at Gram's and the groceries are all carried in.

Gram is putting things away. She has to walk around GrandMin, who is watching everything from her chair parked in the center of the kitchen. "Try them on, Angela," Gram says. "Give us a fashion show. It will make an excuse for me to sit down for a minute."

Angela takes her package to the bathroom and comes back smiling. The shorts look better than she dared to hope. They are shorter than the ones she usually wears, but something about the cut flatters her hips. She does a few silly dance steps to show off.

"Terrific!" her mother says. "I wish I was young enough to wear something like that."

"Well, you're not," Gram says. Angela giggles. She decides to go back to the bathroom and check herself in the long mirror on the back of the closet door. As she leaves the kitchen she hears GrandMin cluck her tongue.

"Who was that girl?" GrandMin asks in a thin, sour voice. "Her legs were bare all the way up."

Angela stops and holds her breath.

"Oh, for heaven's sake, Mother," Gram says. "That's Angela with her new shorts on."

"Now, GrandMin," adds Carol, "all the young girls wear shorts when the weather is hot. Lots of women, too."

Min clears her throat. "I don't like it," she says. "She's young. You'd better watch her."

Angela feels suddenly naked. She goes to the bathroom and changes back into her jeans, won-

dering how she can stand to be here nine more
days.

————

Arminda loved to go walking with Delia because everyone in Jericho took notice when Delia
Walters went walking. Tall as a sunflower, stem
for a waist, she moved like breeze in a garden.

"Evenin', Miss Walters."

"How do, Delia."

"You are a picture tonight, Miss Delia, I do
say."

Min tugged at her sister's hand. "We can go
to the bridge, can't we? Please, can't we?"

"There's no need to squeeze my hand that
way, Min." The older girl pulled away. "People
will think you're sewed onto my sleeve." She
hissed the words between her teeth so that Solo-
mon Coy, whose front porch was close to the
street, wouldn't hear.

"Am I too grown-up to hold your hand?" Min
had been hearing she was too grown for one
thing or another ever since school had begun.
Every day now she trekked across the field to the
Jericho Special District Schoolhouse and took her
seat beside Lucy.

"Six is old enough to know how to act," Delia
went on. "Six is plenty big enough—"

"To go to the creek by myself?" finished Min. The run beside the house had grass clumps full of secrets and a few skating bugs, but Min thought the water must be more interesting in the wide creek beneath the bridge, where she wasn't allowed to go.

"You should've been a boy," Delia said. "I'll bet Wheat wasn't any bit peskier than you when he was little."

"But I'm big," reminded Min. "You said."

"Hush." Delia smoothed her dress and put one hand to the pouf of her hair. One long, seemingly stray curl fell at each temple. She bit her lips fiercely and wet them with her tongue.

"What we coming this way for, Delia?" Min looked with longing toward the bridge on Willow Creek. "Who we going to see down this street? Huh?"

"Hush," Delia said again. "I should have left you up to the cemetery with Lucy and Pa."

Min was silent. She and Lucy could have played hide-and-seek among the headstones. She was better than Lucy at hiding, but not so good with finding. Min liked to stop and feel the letters on the stones, now that she knew what they were, and that took a long time. Sometimes Lucy gave up waiting.

"You needed a walk," Delia said. "Exercise is good for you." And then her eyes went round with something that looked like surprise. "Why, look here, Min," she said. "Here's that handsome Stanley Otterby with nothing to do, just dying to walk a ways with us."

It was Min's turn to say "hush"; she felt certain that Stanley Otterby could hear every word that Delia was saying. He did. He got up from the front step where he had been sitting, put his hands in his pockets, and came along the doorpath toward them.

"Good evening, ladies," he said, and Min liked him because he had big shoulders and a smile in his voice and a clean shirt. He even smelled good. "I hear you are going to school these days, Arminda," he said as he fell into step beside Delia. "Tell me what Mr. Edwards has been teaching a clever little girl like you."

"My letters," said Min. "I read and I spell and I keep a neat slate." Her words came tumbling, and he encouraged her with questions. He talked to Arminda, but his eyes were on Delia.

When the three of them had gone as far as Longwell's orchard, Stanley reached into his pocket and brought out two shiny pennies. "These are yours, Arminda," he said, "if you can find ten windfalls for me."

Delia's cheeks were getting brighter. "Stanley . . ." she began.

"What's the matter?" The young man looked

EVERMAN PUBLIC LIBRARY
11,983

down on Min with mocking eyes. "Can't she count?"

"I can!" Min said defiantly. "I can too count!" She ran off to gather Mr. Longwell's fallen apples in her skirt. On the way home, wanting a pocket, she held Stanley's two pennies tight as extra fingers in her hand.

Wheat was the only one in the house when they got there, and he hooted when Arminda told him how she had earned her money. It was Delia's shoulders that he clasped, however, taking her suddenly from behind and leaning close to her ear. Then he chanted in his sandpaper voice, "Delia, Delia, did he . . ." He glanced over his shoulder at Arminda, grinned, and whispered two more words against Delia's cheek. Quick as a cat, Delia whirled, slapped him, and fled upstairs. But the mark of her hand stayed on his face until bedtime.

4

ANGELA'S BED is on her grandparents' couch, a soft place but too hot for good sleep, even with the fan. Brian is cooler in the basement, she thinks enviously, but then she remembers how stiff the old army cot is and how the smell of cement creeps out of the walls. She adjusts her pillow and pulls her hair to one side. She can't sleep. She has read until her eyes refuse her and now, lights out, she lies awake in a houseful of sleepers.

She hears her great-grandmother stirring, making sounds of discontent in the bedroom just across the entry hall. A few steps from the living room, a few steps more to the bath, Min's room is handy for Gram in the daytime but difficult at night. Whenever Min calls or rings her bell, Kate has to make her way down the steps, clutching the front of her robe with one hand, the stair rail with the other. Sometimes Angela sleeps through Min's night pains and her grandmother's ministrations. Usually she wakes and then pretends to sleep because Gram gets so upset about disturbing her rest. Once when her grandmother was slow to respond to Min's call, Angela went into the old woman's room herself to see if she could help, but Min sent her away.

Now there is quiet again behind the half-closed door, and Angela sits up. She thinks of calling Tessa long distance even though her parents have said that she can surely make do with letters. They do not trust her to talk ten minutes or less, she knows that, but she thinks she could pay her grandfather out of next month's baby-sitting money even if it were a long, long conversation. Tessa has her own phone in her own room and a little cordless TV that she takes to bed with her. She would be awake. She would answer. Longing for her friend's voice, Angela can almost hear it, high and clear, full of laughter. *Don't tell me, I can't stand it! Ange, stop it! It's too funny, Ange, I'm just dying!* She wants to call. Her fingers itch for the phone, but it hangs on the wall near the foot of the stairs, where anyone who wakes might hear her. She sighs. In a few days she will be able to talk to Tessa in the flesh. Maybe she can wait. Maybe she can even get to sleep if she goes into the bathroom and splashes water on her face and arms to cool them.

Angela tiptoes through the hall and feels for

the sink by the glow of Gram's little scallop–shell night-light. The last thing she wants is to wake GrandMin. She nudges the tap for a silent trickle of water, puts her hands in the basin, and waits. From the medicine-chest mirror above, her own shadowed face looks back at her. She leans closer, with a critical eye. Nose too wide, brows too straight, an unfinished face. Someday, she thinks, somewhere, she will look into another face and see her own self clearly, see the person she is going to become. It is a secret expectation. She has never mentioned it, not even to Tessa. Wrists wet, she passes dripping hands across her forehead. Cooler by a fraction, she turns off the water and starts back to the couch.

As Angela pads barefoot past Min's door, the old woman rings her summoning bell. It is a shopkeeper's bell, the kind that sounds a single strident tone when a hand falls on its top; Gram always leaves it within Min's reach. Angela clenches her teeth against the sound, which reminds her of a headache, and pauses in the hallway. Has she wakened GrandMin after all? Min is calling now, but no one upstairs is stirring. Angela hesitates. Sometimes, Gram has said, she is just too tired to wake up in spite of Min's bell. Angela feels a rush of sympathy for her grandmother and decides against going upstairs to get her.

She pushes open Min's door instead. Horizontal slits of moonlight show through the venetian blind and fall in eerie good order across Min's smooth bedcover. Angela tosses her head for courage. Her hair swings below her shoulders.

The old woman whispers, "Delia? Is that you?"

"Who?" Angela steps closer to the bed. "It's me," she says. "Are you all right, GrandMin?"

"Uhhh," Min breathes, as if she has pain. "It's too bright in here. The moon's in my eyes."

"I can fix the blind," Angela offers, relieved. She won't have to wake Gram for this. "Is this better?" She tugs at the cord until the moonlight is nothing but a glitter of threads in the weave of the coverlet. "Okay?"

Min's eyes are closed.

"GrandMin? Is it all right now? Do you need anything else?"

There is no response. Angela bends over the bed, squinting to see. The old woman's face is perfectly still. No air passes her lips, in or out; no twitch disturbs her nostrils. The girl takes a step backward, horrified. *Breathe,* wills Angela silently. *Breathe!* She is conscious of her own heart's ticking, ominous as a clock. But Min lies suspended, paused, in a time of her own.

Angela fights panic. She has to do something. She thinks about putting her hands on her great-grandmother's chest to push, about tilting up her chin to blow into her mouth. Which is right? Both? She can't remember. Her mind races ahead of her body, which feels suddenly numb. When she opens her mouth to scream for her mother, no air comes out.

Finally, desperate, she seizes the ghostly form in the bed by one shoulder. "Breathe!" she pleads in a whisper. "Please, GrandMin, breathe!"

Min breathes. She sucks air in a great gulp and puffs on as if there has been no interruption. Angela is the one who is spent, completely undone. She does not know if Min has come back from the dead or has simply come awake.

Perplexity moves across the old woman's face like another pattern of moon and shadow. "Kate? Is that you?"

"No, GrandMin. It's me. Angela." She releases her great-grandmother's shoulder and steps back from the bed. "I'll get Gram if you need her. Or my mom. I can go upstairs and get Mom."

Min seems not to have heard. "Katy," she says, "wherever did you get that funny nightdress?"

"I'm not Katy," whispers Angela, suddenly conscious of her short ruffled pajamas. "I'm Angela."

"You've been a good mother to me," Min says kindly. "I always wanted a mother. Can you stay, Katy? Can you visit a bit?"

Angela shakes her head, her heart still thumping. She needs to escape. "I'll go get my mother," she says. "Mom likes to talk."

Afterward, after both Gram and Carol have come downstairs to settle GrandMin, Gram assures Angela that Min has had many spells of fitful breathing. It frightens Gram, too, Angela's mother whispers to her as she starts back to her bed. It is one of the reasons Gram needs help, she says, one of the reasons Gram should think, maybe, about a nursing home. Angela nods dutifully without meaning to agree. She lowers herself into the twisted sheets on the couch and squeezes her eyes shut as her mother and grandmother start back upstairs, their low insistent voices layering one over the other. Then Angela sleeps, in spite of the heat, and she does not remember her dreams.

———

"Tell another one, Delia, please." Lucy sat cross-legged on the stair landing where the night

breeze came in, pleading with her soft round
eyes. Min drowsed on the top step with her head
in Delia's lap. She was trying to focus on Lucy's
face, on her fair thin hair lit by starshine, but
Delia's fingers kept winding a curl in and out of
Min's honey-colored strands, and that was the
sleepiest thing in the world.

"You girls ought to go to bed." Delia's voice
was slow and sleepy, too. "If Will comes home
and finds you still up, he'll raise Cain with Pa."

"Pa doesn't care, Delia," Lucy said. "Tell us
the one about the princess grandmother. Please,
please."

Min snuggled against Delia's skirt, which
smelled like the onions she had fried for supper.
"I'm not sleepy," Min lied. "Tell it."

"What little beggars you are." Delia sighed
and nibbled at her lip, but she smiled in the
shadows. "Once upon a time," she began,
"there were two beautiful little girls whose poor
mother had to go to heaven."

Min shut her eyes and let the pictures come
into her head.

"When she got there," Delia said, "her own
mother was waiting, and her mother's mother,
and all those grandmothers all the way back.
And one of those grandmothers had been a . . ."
She paused for effect.

"A princess!" pronounced Lucy. " 'Born in a castle across the sea, high on a mountain where the clouds roll free.' "

"That's good, Lucy," Delia said, approving. "You have a good memory."

Min opened her eyes and sat up. "I have a good memory, too," she said. " 'Born in a castle across—' "

"Arminda, don't poke in," Delia scolded. "You know Lucy likes to help me tell the stories."

Min's mouth fell in a pout, but she allowed herself to be pulled back down into the comfort of Delia's lap.

"Now then," Delia went on. "We don't know her name, but she was a king's daughter. She had more dresses than she could wear and a gold necklace that sparkled when the sun shone on it."

Lucy made a sound of surprise. "Oh," she said, "you never told about the necklace before."

"I just remembered it," Delia said. "Hush, now. One day she was walking in her garden— it was a huge place, you know, just for her, with a little woods and a pond and every flower you could think of—and while she was walking, she heard something."

"An animal?" Min offered.

"It sounded like an animal," agreed Delia. "It sounded like a hurt animal in the woods, and she went to find it because she was so good-hearted and because she was so good at taking care of hurts."

"It wasn't an animal after all," Lucy said confidently. "It was a man—a poor man, a hunter—with a wounded leg. And the princess made him well in no time."

"Don't get ahead of me, now," Delia said. "She washed his wound and bound it up with pieces of her petticoat—linen and silk, I suppose. My, just think of wasting that beautiful material on bandages."

"Then what?" Min pressed.

Lucy snorted. "Then they fell in love, silly."

Min stuck out her tongue. Outside, the *clop-rattle-clop, clop-rattle-clop* of a horse and carriage grew louder.

"Hurry, Delia," Lucy said. "It's Will."

"They did fall in love." Delia's voice rushed on. "But her father was angry about it and sent the hunter away, so she was very sad. Then one night, when she thought she would have to spend her whole life in that castle, lonely forever, the hunter came back for her, and they ran off together. She never saw the castle again, and she didn't care."

"Did she miss her father?" Min asked.

"I'll bet she took the necklace with her," Lucy said.

Delia stood up. "I don't know. All I know is they loved each other and lived together until they died, and one of their children was a grand-mother of ours, way, way back."

Min stood up and hugged Delia's waist. "And it's true, too, isn't it? Every word."

Lucy snorted. "Our mother used to tell that story, Min. Except Delia tells it better, I bet. When she doesn't have to rush, anyway."

"Hurry, now," Delia said. "I just have time to tuck you."

The sheet on the bed Min shared with Lucy was thin as paper. Delia pulled it smooth over the two of them and secured it so tightly that their toes bent. She stood for a moment, looking down at them and then at her hands, with all the calluses and rough spots that had caught and picked the fine stuff of the sheet. "Just imagine," she said to her hands, "being in love and going away and having your own life."

Lucy wiggled her toes to loosen the cover. "What did you say?"

"Nothing. You two get to sleep."

Min closed her eyes. She could hear her fa-ther's snoring and her brother's boots clattering on the porch. Lucy lay beside her as familiar as a twin. But it was Delia who was comfort, even after she had swished her long skirts out of the bedroom and down the dark stairs.

5

ANGELA SLEEPS LATE and wakens confused, not yet remembering the night just past. Voices from the kitchen drift through the fuzziness in her head and begin to sort themselves out: Gram, GrandMin, a neighbor woman, a child. Quickly now Angela rolls off the couch, wads up her sheets, and stuffs them under the cushions, out of sight. The visitors probably walked right past her, she thinks. They must have seen her puffy face and tangled hair. She feels violated. It takes a moment to know the voice: a woman named Virginia, who is much younger than Angela's parents. Virginia lives alone with her little boy, who is five and says rude things whether or not his mother is listening.

Angela barely has time to sneak upstairs and pull on some clothes in the bedroom her parents use before he comes looking for her. "Go away, Garth," she says as she tries to smooth her hair.

She is thinking about GrandMin now, and she really wants privacy.

"You've got bed head," he says in his high, thin voice, and then, taunting, "I ate your pancakes. Your grandma said I could."

Angela shrugs. She isn't hungry anyway. She remembers that when they first came to Gram's, she had hoped to baby-sit for this child. Now she is relieved that his mother can't afford it. "Come on downstairs now," she says, certain that Gram would not want him to look in every closet, as he has started to do.

In the kitchen she is surprised that all seems routine. Angela looks sidelong at her great-grandmother to see if she bears any mark of last night's problem. The old woman sits in her wheelchair with tea and crackers on her tray, just as she has done every morning. She seems not to see Angela. Her eyes are on Virginia's chattering mouth, but it is hard to tell if she is listening.

Gram smiles a welcome in Angela's direction and offers orange juice with a slice of banana bread.

"Virginia brought this," Gram says. "I don't know what I'd do without good neighbors."

"Good morning, sugar," Virginia says, and goes right on telling GrandMin how smart Garth is turning out to be.

Angela smiles a tight little smile. She hates

banana bread and doesn't want to hear about Garth. Still, she is grateful that no one has mentioned the exact time, which is closer to lunch than breakfast.

"Hurry a little, Angel," Gram says as Angela picks at the food. "Your mom wants you to help Brian carry some boxes from the attic at the other house." Her voice is quiet so as not to rise above Virginia's one-sided conversation with GrandMin. "You can just put them out there on the back porch, and we'll sort through them later."

Angela welcomes this assignment as an excuse to leave.

"Don't be surprised to find a stranger in the back," Gram says as Angela puts her glass in the sink. "Your grandfather hired a boy to help trim up the bushes and get the yard in shape."

Suddenly GrandMin is listening. "What yard?" she says abruptly.

"Who's the boy?" Virginia wants to know.

"Your yard, Mother," Gram says. "And it's one of the Ferris kids. The middle one."

"That one?" Virginia giggles. "Tom Ferris? He's going to be such a hunk when he grows up, don't you think?"

GrandMin's spoonful of tea stops on the way to her mouth. "Does he steal?" she asks. "I bet he steals. He'll be up to no good."

"They say he's a good worker," Gram tells her, and Angela hears the deliberate patience in her voice. "His dad takes care of the cemetery now, and the boy does all the trimming."

Angela closes her eyes for a moment. Of all the people she does not want to see this morning, the boy from the cemetery tops the list.

"Hurry now," Gram says to her. She pats Angela's back with a slender, worn hand.

Angela goes, reluctantly, across the lawn to the house that was GrandMin's home as a child and for most of her long life. It seems dumpy to Angela, a frazzled old house with a half story on top that used to be bedrooms but is really nothing more than an attic. She avoids the flagstone path that leads to the back door and circles to the front, where her father and grandfather are painting. They are sweating and silent, although the radio is blaring. Her mother is inside, in GrandMin's dining room, smearing wallpaper sizing with its foul smell up and down the wall.

"You can start hauling those boxes over to Gram's any time now," Carol directs. Angela holds her nose and decides not to complain about the lack of a greeting. Her mother's face is pink, working toward fuchsia.

"Okay. Sure." Angela can hear Brian's feet upstairs and the muffled boom of exaggerated bass from his radio. There is no sign of anyone who might be Tom Ferris. She moves on to the kitchen, where she checks the back windows and is relieved to see no one.

The waiting cartons are dark with dust and smudged by her brother's fingers. What could all this stuff be? she wonders. Its oldness weighs on her spirit. She picks up two of the smaller boxes, thinking she can manage, but the smell affects her. A dead, musty odor clings to the cardboard and blows into her face as she steps down onto the back stoop, aiming for the walk. Her nose twitches, her eyes squeeze shut of their own accord, and a great sneeze explodes out of her mouth. She is blinded just long enough to lose her footing. She twists her ankle and goes sprawling so quickly that there is no time to cry out. Both boxes bounce out of her grasp, and their contents spill across the old well curb beside the walk. She grabs her knee, which is bleeding a little, and under her breath says a couple of Tessa's favorite words.

She hears Brian yell something just as she sees the boy from the cemetery loping toward her. "You all right?" he calls. Angela wants to shrink away to nothing. What he really wants to know, she thinks, is why she is so clumsy.

"I missed the step," she says to Brian, who gets there first and stands looking down at her, shaking his head.

"What a genius." He pulls her to her feet with one hand.

"I'm fine, though." She bites her lip because her knee is throbbing. She tries not to look at the other boy, who has stooped to gather the envelopes and pictures and tiny boxes tied with string that are jumbled in the grass.

"Look at this old guy," he says, tilting a bent photograph toward the sun. "Must have been having a bad day."

Brian snorts in appreciation. "Look at that one by your foot." Both boys laugh like conspirators at something Angela does not see, and she feels suddenly protective.

"Don't make fun," she says. "They're all dead, probably."

"Don't be such a buffalo." Brian glares, but the other boy studies her.

"I guess you're Angela," he says. "I'm Tom." He is so close to her as he hands up the first box that she can see the individual hairs on his arm and the sweat marks on his T-shirt and the exact color of his eyes, an icy gray. She takes a big breath to get rid of a feeling that comes over her, one she doesn't recognize and doesn't quite like.

It is Brian who takes the box and says the thank you, and then Angela realizes that he must have met Tom already and talked to him. She considers what they might have said about her, and all of the speculations are painful. She mumbles her own thanks, picks up the other box, and struggles to give them a dignified rear view as she walks away. What is it about boys that makes life so complicated, she wonders, and wishes hard for Tessa, who probably knows.

———

"Go on, you two," Delia said to her sisters. "Supper's all put away now, so you can go play." She took off her apron and folded it with a snap. "Or take the basket and see if there's any more hickory nuts back along the run. I don't care which."

Lucy let her face go long. "What you going to do, Delia?"

"Read or something, maybe. Mending. I don't know." Delia squared her thin shoulders. "I might even take a rest."

Arminda tossed her head. "In your Sunday waist?" she asked.

Delia's hand went up to her ruffled neckpiece and fell down the row of tiny, shining buttons to her skirt. "You two have fussed and complained this whole day, and I'm sick of it," she said swiftly. "You go on out and do whatever you like." She pointed. "But do it right now."

They went.

It was getting on into October, the glow of the

year. The maples on the far side of the run were bright as butter, their trunks twined with scarlet ivy. It was Min's favorite time. She didn't even mind being put out of the house; nothing inside was as fine as autumn. "Autumn" was a new word from her school reader. It sounded much better than "fall," she thought, much more grown. It made everyone notice how forward she was for eight years old. "I love autumn," she said out loud.

"Oh, shush," Lucy said. "Quit your putting on airs."

"Lucy Goosey," taunted Min. "Been sucking on a lemon."

Lucy scowled at her. "Our mama is probably grieving in heaven this very minute to hear you make fun of the beautiful name she gave me. Sometimes I think you're as wicked as Wheat."

The words stung. "Wheat is not either wicked," Min said stoutly. "He's just high-spirited." She had heard her father say so when he was explaining to the new preacher why it was that Wheat had one short finger. Wheat and the Ziler twins were acting the fool at the church woodpile when Wheat put his finger on the block and dared Henry Ziler to chop it off. Henry raised up the ax, just pretending, but Hiram jostled his arm. Down came the ax blade and off came the end of Wheat's finger. Wheat had bled like a stuck hog, Pa said, but he had laughed as much as he hollered. Min thought that was brave, not wicked.

A puff of wind rattled through dry bushes at the edge of the garden plot, lonely sounding. "Don't be mad at me, Lucy," Min said. "Let's go up to the cemetery and help Pa."

Lucy wrapped her arms around her chest. "I'd rather be in by the stove," she said. "Like Delia. I don't know why we can't stay in when she does. We have to leave because we might disturb her—honestly! Like we were little kids. You might make noise, Min, but I wouldn't. I'm ten years old."

Min arranged her face to show that she was insulted, but it didn't last. She didn't like for anyone to criticize Delia. "Don't be cross with Delia, Lucy. She made biscuits and everything tonight. And she wore that pretty waist with all the buttons that makes her look so nice." She tugged at Lucy's hand. "Let's go up where Pa is," she said again. "We can run and that will keep you warm." She danced ahead, clutching at her skirt, urging Lucy on.

Together they crossed the field and ran toward the hill. Halfway up, along the road's edge where the stones were sharp, Min fell and skinned her knee. Much as she bit her lip, she couldn't keep from crying. Bright drops of blood oozed out of her stocking.

"You'd better go down to the pump and wash that off," Lucy said, when Min had quit sniffling, "or there'll be a big bloody smear on the front of your skirt." She held the worn plaid away from Min's leg with two fingers.

"Come help me." Min rubbed her nose with the back of her hand. "Please."

"Oh, for heaven's sake, Min. You can take care of yourself. I'm going on up and practice my speaking piece for Pa."

"Wait for me, then," Min begged. "I'll hurry." She loved the way Lucy recited the poem about Hiawatha's childhood, loved the strange-sounding words and the steady rocking of her sister's dreamy voice, loved to think of "the shining Big-Sea-Water," so different from Willow Creek. "Don't start till I get back," she said.

Half running, half hopping, Arminda went back toward the house alone—through the field, along the edge of the garden plot, into the dooryard. The well water was cold. It took away some of the stinging in her knee, but the blood still beaded up slowly and seeped through her stocking. She ought to get a rag, she thought, and tie it around her knee so there wouldn't be spots on her dress. There were rags in the catchall just inside the kitchen door, and it wouldn't take more than a minute to get one. She would be so quiet that Delia would never hear.

Min walked stiff-legged to the door and pushed softly. Nothing happened. She frowned and twisted the knob. It wouldn't turn. The latch must have slipped, she thought. Doors in Jericho were never locked unless someone was making a long, long visit far from home. She hopped off the back step and sidled along the house till she came to the parlor window. Its catch broken, it slid up and down easily from outside. Even if Delia was taking a nap, Min thought, she could still creep in and make a bandage. She tucked her skirt into her drawers and stood on tiptoe to raise the sash as high as she could. No squeak- ing—that was good. Then she hooked her hands over the sill and pulled herself up, head and shoulders in, bottom and legs dangling out. Her skirt was caught somewhere on a splinter, and as she tugged it loose her eyes adjusted to the dimness of the room.

The parlor door was open, and in the hallway beyond was Delia. Arminda caught her breath and held it. There was Delia standing in the hall- way. With a man. He was pressed up tight against her, kissing and kissing. Delia's hair hung free below her shoulders. Her skirt was crooked.

Min opened her mouth to call out. *Stop!* she cried in her mind. *Don't you hurt Delia!* But something new inside her made her silent. She watched without a word, and when she was full of watching she slid backward over the sill and brought the window down with one hand.

"Just look at your dress!" Lucy scolded when she met Min on the hill. "It's smeared worse than if you'd never fixed it."

"I don't care." Min had forgotten about her knee.

"And what took you so long? I recited my piece two whole times and you missed them both."

"I don't care," Min said again. "I hate it anyway."

"Sassypants," said Lucy, wanting explanation. But she searched her sister's fathomless eyes in vain.

6

SUNDAY AFTERNOON descends like sleep on Gatesville. GrandMin snores gently in her bed, reassuringly noisy. Even Gram is working in the old house, so Angela stands watch alone, waiting for the creeping hands of the clock to catch up to her ideas. She has already reread the best of her mother's books and is beginning to feel desperate. Eyes open, she dreams of home. At four, she knows, if GrandMin sleeps that long, and if the others don't come looking for lemonade, at four she will perform a liberating act.

At 3:45 she can wait no longer. She pulls her hair behind her ears and goes to the telephone in the hallway. "I'd like to make a collect call," she says, giving her name as quietly as she can. She repeats Tessa's number from memory. Be there, she whispers to herself. Take my call. Please, Tessa.

For one heart-stopping moment Angela thinks

it is Tessa's mother who answers, but then an operator says, "Go ahead, please."

"Ange? Is it really you?" The voice squeals on the last word.

"I'll pay you back for this, honest," Angela says first, and then, "Tessa, it's so boring here and I miss you so much. I just had to talk to you."

"I miss you, too. It sounds awful from your letter, Ange. Is your old grandmother still alive?"

"Alive? Sure." Now that the familiar voice is in her ear, Angela's own words turn small. She can't find what it is she wants to say.

"Did your parents get their project done so you can come home?"

"Not yet. But this is Dad's last vacation week."

Tessa giggles. "Have them leave Brian there to finish up. No, wait—I don't mean that. Brian's cute."

"Tessa, what are you saying?" Angela's throat begins to form a giggle of her own. She feels better. "Are we talking about Brian the burper here?" They both laugh, and Tessa begins to talk about everything and nothing so that Angela needs only to say "Mmm" or "C'mon" or "Tess, no!" to keep her going. For a moment it is as good as home.

"Ange, were you serious when you said there wasn't anyone our age where you are? Really?"

"Really."

There is a tiny click which might be Tessa's sympathy or Tessa's call waiting, Angela isn't sure, but it allows her to go on. "Well," she says, "there is only one boy I've met who helped a little bit at GrandMin's house, but he's older than we are, I think."

Tessa gives a whoop. "Go for it," she advises. "You need entertainment."

"What do you *mean*?" Angela's tone is protest, but every word nourishes her. Tessa makes her feel normal, alive.

"You know, talk to him. Find out about him. You don't have to *do* anything."

"Tessa, I don't want to talk to him. Every time I see him I do something really stupid. And no telling what Brian has told him about me."

"There you go with negative thinking again. What does he look like, anyway? Is he ugly?"

"No." Angela makes a picture of Tom Ferris in her mind, which is exciting in a weird way. He isn't ugly. "Oh, I don't know. I'd just feel funny starting up a conversation with him. He helps take care of the cemetery."

"Gross." Tessa's voice is cheerful. "Stephen King stuff. I'd love it. Take notes for me. What did you say he looks like?"

The back screen slams, and the receiver nearly slips from Angela's hand. "I have to go," she whispers.

"What? Oh, I wish you didn't. Remember, now, think positive. You need *someone* to talk to. Friends forever, Ange."

"I miss you, Tess. G'bye."

Brian peers in from the dining room. "Who was that?"

Angela wants to say "None of your business," but she thinks better of it. "Just Tessa," she says with nonchalance, and then quickly, "I called collect."

"That motor-mouth? Mom will have a fit if she finds out you called her."

"She won't either. Mom likes Tessa." Angela wants this to be true, but she knows her mother's view of Tessa really has more to do with tolerance than affection.

Brian rolls his eyes. "Women!" he says.

They are faced off there by the telephone when they hear Min in the bedroom. "Who's there?" she calls. "Who's there?"

Brian turns to go, but Angela grabs the front of his shirt. "Go in with me," she whispers.

"Wimp," he says in her ear, but he does go to the doorway with her to stand where GrandMin can see him.

Min's blinds are shut against the afternoon

light. "Who is that?" she says, moving her head a little.

"Just me, GrandMin." Brian speaks in the cheerful voice he uses for everyone but Angela. "I came to get some ice water."

The old woman's mouth makes a crooked curve like an egg cracking. "Why, it's Brian," she says. "Come sit with me."

"No, GrandMin, I can't. I have to get back to work." He takes his first step backward. "But how are you? Are you feeling okay?"

"I'm just the same," she says. "I'm always just the same. I don't know why I can't die now."

"Uh-huh." Brian slips out of sight, pushing Angela to the front.

Min considers her in silence. "Did you know that my folks are all gone?" she says at last, and Angela sighs. She is trying to hear the echo of Tessa's lively voice, but it isn't there.

————

Before the trees budded, Delia got fat and went away with her suitcase. Will took her in the wagon, driving with a heavy hand and a face like Judgment Day. Right away Lucy took over the cooking and the job of telling Min what to do. Peel the potatoes, Min. Cut me a dab of butter, Min. This is enough salt, isn't it, Min? You put the plates around and I'll call Pa.

Min was grumpy. "When is Delia coming back?" she asked on the second lonely night. "She's coming back, isn't she, Lucy?"

"Maybe." Lucy let go of a troubled breath. "Maybe not."

"But Will just took her for a little visit with Aunt Clara, didn't he? Why wouldn't she come back?"

"Because," Lucy said.

Arminda stomped an angry foot. "Because why not?"

"Because she had to go way up in the country where nobody knows her, is why."

The thought of Delia in a far place made a catch in Min's throat. She was careful not to cry. She was getting too old to cry. It was Lucy who finally sat at the table and sobbed, letting the potatoes burn.

"Don't you tell, Min," she said. "Don't tell that I know, or Will might take the strap to me." She leaned close to her sister's ear. "Delia went off to have a baby. That's why she wore her apron all the time, to hide herself sticking out in front like that."

"But," protested Min, "but she . . . There isn't any father."

"Don't be such a goose." Lucy wiped her eyes fiercely on her long, bedraggled sleeve. "Every baby has a father. Delia just isn't married to him, that's all."

Min's eyes were round and still.

"Will says she's a fallen woman," Lucy went on, "and it would be wicked for her to stay here. I'll just bet that's something Ermabeth Frazey told him to say."

Min nodded slowly. She knew Miss Ermabeth Frazey, who was going to get married to Will, maybe, and who knew what was right and wrong about everything. Min didn't know what it meant to be a fallen woman, but she felt something lost and shameful in it. Her shoulders began to ache with the lack of Delia's arm to draw her close. Her head felt light, knowing that Delia wouldn't be there to do her hair with ribbons. No more stories. She felt like crying. Instead, she went to the stove and tugged the smoking skillet off the fire.

"I like babies," she said. "And poop on old Ermabeth Frazey."

"Arminda!" Lucy said. "You mind your language."

And then they both wept.

7

ANGELA IS ON HER WAY, by choice, to the cemetery. She is amazed at herself for taking Tessa's advice—*Go for it! Talk to him*—but anything seems better to her today than staying in to hear the old voice and the old words. She is proud of herself for being so clever in making her escape from Gram's, and almost embarrassed that it has been so easy. In her hand is a new spiral-bound notebook that Grandpa found for her in a desk drawer. Large calligraphy letters, her mother's contribution, spell out *Family History*. Her father has said he is thankful to see her take an interest in something. Only Brian has laughed, but she doesn't care because it gives her such pleasure to deceive him.

She has said that she will copy down the inscriptions on all the family gravestones, names and dates and whatever else is there. Last year her teacher suggested this as a social studies project. Angela thought, still thinks, that this is an incredibly boring idea. At the time she moaned and giggled about it with Tessa while they decided on another project. But now she sees possibilities in this lifeless activity—an excuse for getting away from GrandMin, a reason for talking to the boy, a plot to share with Tessa. Tessa loves plots.

In the notebook Gram has drawn a map and made a neat list of surnames for which Angela should search. "It's too bad Min can't help you with this," Gram has told her. "Sam Walters— he was Min's father—was the cemetery caretaker years and years ago. She and her sister Lucy grew up playing hide-and-go-seek around the tombstones."

Angela thinks of this now as she consults Gram's drawing and tries to remember which way she turned to deliver the jar of flowers last week. Even when she concentrates, she cannot imagine little girls in long dresses running here, crouching and hopping up, shouting "Here I come, ready or not!" Maybe the modern drone of the power mower on the other side of the hill blocks her imagination. The sound makes her smile, though. Tom Ferris might be here. She goes to look for him, to ask directions to the Walters family stone, although she can see it now as plain as gasoline signs along the interstate. Tessa would be proud.

She is just raising her arm to wave at the figure on the little tractor, just forming a shout of "Hey, Tom," just feeling that maybe she can do this, when she realizes something is not right. The person who is mowing has a beard. He is old enough to be her father. What if he sees her? She gets a panicky stomach. Her earlobes begin to feel hot. She wishes that she could blush like other people, with red cheeks instead of red ears. Clutching the notebook to her chest, she retraces her steps, feeling stupid for being in the cemetery at all.

Angela is walking fast, trying to decide if this could all be Tessa's fault, when she realizes that she cannot go back to Gram's with an empty notebook. She dodges from gravestone to gravestone to the one marked Walters, hoping the man on the tractor will not look her way. She tries to ignore the sun, which seems to grow brighter by the minute, striking once on the back of her head and a second time in her eyes as it glares off the first white page. She squints as she writes *Samuel B. 1850–1923; Mary M. 1856–1895.* In spite of herself she computes their ages. Circling the stone, which has the shape of an obelisk, she discovers names carved on all four sides: William, Lillian, Jesse, Charles, another Mary.

Strangers. Mystery people. A quiver of interest comes and then fades as she writes hastily, not bothering to dot the i's. Tom Ferris and his weird job. Why doesn't he work in some civilized place? She wishes that Gatesville had an ice-cream store for Tom Ferris to work in. Or a McDonald's. Her mind drifts home, where fast food is plentiful.

Preoccupied, Angela bumps her toe against a small, worn stone hidden in the droop of an overgrown peony. She has to get down on her knees to read the inscription: S.W. 1900–1902. Her breath sucks in of its own accord. This is just a little child. Her imagination goes to work, and her eyes fill up and threaten to spill over, as if she were reading a sad novel.

She has had enough of this cemetery, she thinks, closing her notebook. She hurries toward the gate. But Tom Ferris is just now on his way in, pedaling fast on an old bicycle. A younger boy, a Tom Ferris look-alike, races along behind, on foot. "Wait up!" he yells. "Tom! Wait up!" Angela's reflexes get her out of the way before they have a chance to run over her.

"Hey!" Tom calls to her. "What're you doing here?"

It occurs to Angela that she doesn't have to answer. The rider and runner clatter on by, and she hears the smaller version of Tom, trying to keep his voice low: "Is she the one? Is she?"

Angela is completely still. The one *what*? He has been talking about her. Her ears go from crimson to scarlet, and they are still pinker than normal when she gets back to Gram's.

———

The year Min's father had spring pneumonia, he told Will that the Lord had sent him a vision: two angels that sat on the wagon-shed roof and talked as plain as anything. *If you would live, Sam Walters,* the holy visitors said, *gather your children. Gather your children.* Jesse had gone to the great West to make his fortune, too far away to be gathered. But Delia could come home, their father insisted, and the child could come with her.

And so Arminda became a second mother to little Sammy. She was twelve and ready for it, but ready or not, it had to be. Delia worked six days out of seven at the hotel in town, sharing a bedroom at Sardo's boardinghouse with another of the kitchen girls. Even on the days she came home to Jericho, she had little time for Sammy.

"Land, he just wears me out," she would say. "You watch him, Min." And then she would stretch out on the daybed with a novel, unless Will was there. He berated her for reading trash. Usually she stayed out of Will's sight anyway, because Ermabeth Frazey was still scandalized about Delia's baby. She kept telling Will she just couldn't see how a respectable woman like herself could marry into the Walters family.

Arminda squeezed Sammy in a hug every time he came close to her. My, but she loved him. And he thought the world of her. Everyone could see it.

"Mim! Mim!" he would call from his bed in the morning, and "Mim! Mim!" from his high wooden chair in the kitchen, piping for attention like a round baby bird. He never called for Lucy, Min thought with satisfaction. Lucy was too dreamy to hear him anyway. Now that she had fallen head over heels for Edgar Otterby, she often stood moon-eyed over her kitchen tasks, spending an hour on five minutes' work. Lucy even borrowed Delia's novels and read them in the pantry, where Will never came. But Arminda had Sammy.

It was autumn and the pears were ripe. "I pick," Sammy said when he saw her get the basket. "I pick, too."

"No, you play in here." She was tying a scarf around her hair. "The wind might give you the earache."

"Huh-uh, no, Mim. No, huh-uh." He shook his head so fast that Min was afraid he would addle his brain. Besides, she couldn't resist him.

"Come on, then," she said, looking for a knit cap among Wheat's old things in the cupboard. "Pull this down tight and don't you dare run off." He was such a care sometimes; no telling what he might get into if you didn't think ahead. Arminda squared her shoulders.

"You can get some pears for Grandpa," she said as they walked into the long grass at the edge of the orchard. "Pickled pears are Grandpa's favorite." And that's what I'm going to make, she thought. Not Lucy. Just me. She hurried, picking from the low branches and sorting quickly through the fallen fruit. Firm pears were best for pickling, Delia had said. She hoped there wouldn't be too many rotten spots to cut out. She culled mostly by touch because she had to keep her eyes on Sammy. The fragrance of soft pears, ripe and too-ripe pears, rose up all around her, a gold smell, very sweet.

Sammy ran to the next tree and wrinkled his nose. "Dumpling!" he announced. "Smell dumpling!"

Arminda laughed, and the moment caught and fixed itself in her mind. She thought she would remember it forever—the child's face beaming beneath his oversize cap, the sun barely warm through the thinning leaves, the heavy perfume of pears. Then suddenly there was a stab of pain in her hand so fierce that she dropped her basket. As the fruit went rolling, a yellow jacket fell away from the tender flesh between her thumb and forefinger.

"Eeee!" she screeched, cradling the injury with her other hand. "Ow! *Ow!* I got stung!"

Sammy began to wail in sympathy. "Ooo! I coming, Mim! I coming." His short legs churned through grass and pears until a slippery spot sent him tumbling.

Arminda rubbed at her hand and whispered two of Wheat's cuss words as she started for Sammy. Now she would have to clean him up as well as gather the spilled fruit; there wouldn't be time to get started on anything else before the men came in for dinner.

All at once the little boy screamed, his voice so urgent and off-key that Arminda flung herself toward him. "Sammy! What's the matter? Sammy!"

He had fallen into a feasting of yellow jackets. They were drunk on pear nectar, spoiling to fight. There were too many of them to count, clinging wickedly to his neck and face and chubby hands and to the bare knee that showed above one stocking. Arminda screamed on his behalf, feeling his pain, and for herself, terrified that she would not be able to help him.

"Oh, Sammy, baby!" She tried to brush the devils away as she picked him up, but the ones that left him began to strike her. Finally she snatched off her scarf and chased them with that, then wrapped it over Sammy's head as she ran for the house. When they were out of the territory of pears, the yellow jackets lost interest, but Sammy screamed on.

Arminda had eleven stings, Sammy had too many. She and Lucy bathed him in soda water and sent Wheat into town with the wagon to get Delia and the doctor, who brought a salve that helped. Sammy's whimpering ceased, and he fell asleep on the daybed with gauze wrappings that made him look lumpy and unfamiliar. Min sat beside him and ignored the pain that kept throbbing back into her hands in spite of the medicine.

It was misery to see the slits that were Sammy's eyes and the little puffed cheeks that wanted no food. Not Sammy, Min kept thinking, not Sammy. She thought she should never have let him go out with her. But in two days he was better, sitting up and wanting custard. Delia went back to the hotel, and as the swelling in Arminda's hands subsided, she began to feel happy again.

Through all the trouble Min's father was sad but stoic. He was always careful not to show an unseemly depth of feeling for Delia's out-of-wedlock child. Still, Sammy was his first grandson, and his namesake. It was easy to see the enormity of his relief when the little boy rallied.

"That little dickens," Sam said. "He's a tough little bird like his grandpa. We're out of the woods now, Min."

The very next week Sammy took a fever and lay for days between sleep and death, until Min's love for him was almost lost in her exhaustion at being his nurse. On the fourth morning, before first light had given way to sunrise, his shallow breathing became no breath at all.

The common wisdom in Jericho was that Delia's child had died of the yellow-jacket stings. The doctor said he died of a fever. Whatever the medical truth, Sammy's death called attention to his life. Old gossip came to the funeral. Delia, in black, seemed not to hear the echoes that sounded from Mrs. Otterby's declarations of sympathy, or Ermabeth Frazey's sad clucking. Still, whenever she raised her head, there was something fierce behind her red-rimmed eyes.

The mound of fresh-turned earth on Sammy Walters's little grave had not yet begun to settle when Delia packed her clothes. She was going to California, she announced, to live a life of her own.

"Got a man already picked out, I'd bet," said Will, who was not given to grief or sympathy, either one.

"Delia, girl, don't go," her father begged. They argued it for days, Will and Sam and Delia, but in the end Delia went.

Lucy took to her bed. The housework was all up to Min, and though she scoffed at Lucy for putting on airs, she was glad to be busy. Using the carpet beater brought her such comfort that she cleaned all the rugs twice in one week. Yet there were moments to stop and think, and then she felt empty as a cup.

Life was a wonder, she thought one day in the middle of mending a petticoat. It was so full of partings, so lonely, that it was a puzzle why people should cling to it. She rubbed the hard little sting bumps on her hand and set her jaw and didn't cry. She was twelve, but she felt very old. The next day she began putting down all her hems.

8

ANGELA KNOWS by the bicycle leaning against the tree that Tom must be helping Brian this afternoon at GrandMin's house, although she can see no one. She is stuck inside at Gram's, actually needed for once. Her father and grandfather have gone fishing so as not to waste Jay's vacation in its absolute entirety, as he has been saying pointedly for several days. Mom is finishing the last of the wallpapering at Min's, claiming relief at being rid of her husband's radio. And Gram is doing laundry in the basement. She lugs it up the steps to dry outside on the line because, she says, sun is always better than bleach.

Angela has a list of things Gram wants her to do while Min is in bed: wash the dishes from lunch and put them away, sweep off the front porch, bundle the newspapers in the pantry and tie them with string. She is glad for these things to do with her hands. Without chores she would have nothing to do but stare at the calendar.

After today there are only two tomorrows; Sunday they will go home. Seventy-two hours, she thinks, and feels the burden of each one shifting toward anticipation.

Finally Angela is feeling a little bit good. Over the dishes she makes plans in her head for the rest of the summer. She thinks about the stories she will tell Tessa about these last weeks, which have come to seem a fraction less oppressive now that they are almost over. From time to time she glances out the window to check the bicycle in the next yard. Not that she cares whether it's there, she tells herself. It is something like a zit—unsightly, but impossible to ignore.

She watches the bicycle and daydreams, imagining Tom Ferris and that younger boy, who she thinks must be his brother. What did they say about her? How would she ever know? She is halfway to her elbows in dishwater, thinking instead of washing, when she hears an odd sound.

"GrandMin?" Angela calls, but there is no answer. "Gram?"

The sound comes again, louder. *Thump! Crash!*
"GrandMin?"

"Ohh!" And again, "ohhh!"

Angela sprints toward the bedroom, wiping suds on her blouse. She hears her grandmother from the basement stairs, calling, "What's happened? What's wrong?"

Angela is first to Min's door, first to see the old woman in a heap beside her bed. Her nightchair, a big wooden potty chair for adults, is fallen behind her, leaking a slow puddle on the rug. Angela hesitates. "GrandMin—"

Gram is at her elbow now. "Mother!" Kate rushes past Angela to crouch over the form on the floor. "Are you all right?" She pulls the skirt of Min's housecoat over her puffy, dimpled knees.

Angela doesn't want to look. She tugs the fallen chair upright, wrinkling her nose in expectation of a terrible odor, but there isn't one.

Kate is patting the old woman's shoulder. "Are you all right, Mother? Do you hurt anywhere?"

"I didn't break anything," Min says, her voice surprisingly strong. "I know I didn't. I can tell."

Angela's heart thumps a beat of relief. She watches now as her grandmother checks GrandMin's legs and arms, feeling carefully for damage.

"Thank goodness you've still got strong bones," Gram says, and then, "What were you trying to do, Mother?"

"I had to go," Min says.

Gram shakes her head. "Whyever didn't you ring your bell?" Angela wonders how she manages to keep her voice as patient as her touch.

"The bell is right here where it always is, and you knew Angela would come and get me."

"I was going by myself." Min's eyes focus on something far away.

"You know you mustn't." Frustration begins to creep into Gram's voice. "This is what happens. You know it; it's happened before. And it's so hard to get you—" She quits talking in the middle of her sentence and lets go of a big sigh.

"Can I help?" whispers Angela. She feels somehow like an intruder.

"I can do it, I think, Angel," Gram says. "I know how to manage her. If she can get over onto her knees and take hold of the end of the bed, she can help pull herself up. I've done it before." Gram takes a breath. "You go get some of those old towels in the bottom of the cupboard there in the bathroom—you know where I mean."

Angela goes to the cupboard and is trying to decide whether Gram wants the plain yellow towels or the pink flowered ones when she hears a new commotion in the bedroom. First comes one voice of distress and then another, suddenly too alike to separate. Angela grabs any old towel and hurries back across the hall.

GrandMin is still flat on the floor, her face troubled. "Poor Katy," she says. Gram sits awkwardly beside her, clutching one ankle.

"You'd better go get somebody, Angel," says Gram in an unfamiliar tone. "I think I've done something to myself."

This unthinkable thing settles like a stone in Angela's mind. All her concern for her grandmother cannot block the first thoughts: How will they get along without Gram? Who will take care of GrandMin now? She stands frozen like a child playing at statues.

"Poor Katy," says Min again from the floor. "You'd better come home with me. They'll look after us there." Her eyes glitter.

"Angela!" says Gram sharply. It is a name she seldom uses, and the sound of it rouses Angela to action. Gram is hurting now.

"I'll get Mom," she says. She runs out of the house and across both yards, shouting: "Mom! Brian! Mom! Gram's hurt!"

Poor Gram, Angela thinks, and then, poor us. Her eyes get teary; things blur. But she doesn't have to see clearly to know her mother's panic. Carol leaves a strip of new wallpaper dangling and rushes for the other house, hands still slithery with paste. Brian dashes past them with Tom Ferris in tow.

Angela has no room to think about Tom until the rescue operation is almost over. Gram is carried to the living-room couch, at her own insistence, in a human chair the boys make by joining hands. Carol's protest that they should call for an ambulance because Gram's ankle might be broken goes unheeded. Brian figures a way to get GrandMin back into bed, with his mother's help and Tom's.

"You kids stay with her for a minute," Carol says after the three have struggled to lift Min, with eventual success. "Make sure she stays put while I see about your grandmother."

Angela, who has been trying to stay out of the way, is suddenly conscious that Tom is still here, an outsider in a very private place. She is embarrassed that he should be seeing the stack of disposable bed pads on Min's dresser and the wet stain on her rug. She wants to say, "Thanks for helping—you can go now," but she can't do that. She hides behind her hair.

Min's breathing measures out a moment of awkwardness when no one has anything to say. Then it is Brian who speaks. "I'll bet we don't get to go home Sunday."

"Of course we'll go home," hisses Angela, but she knows better. Their mother won't be able to leave, not now. Brian will be right.

Tom looks so straight at Angela that she has to study her shoes. "Maybe you'll get to like it here," he says. "Maybe you'll want to stay all summer."

Angela has her mouth all ready to protest,

"Don't be silly, I don't want to be trapped here," when she glances up into his see-through eyes. She is suddenly as elated as she was in kindergarten when she realized that she could read, because Tom Ferris seems just now, for an instant, as clear to her as words on a page. I get it, she thinks. He likes me.

Min stirs. "Say," she says, "are we in Jericho yet? Are we home?"

"It's Gatesville, GrandMin," Angela says quickly, hoping that Brian has not noticed Tom's look. "You're always home."

Min lets her thin lips fall into a pout. "I am not," she says, and turns her face away.

Behind Tom, Brian grins at Angela and makes exaggerated silent kisses in the air.

———

One package came from Delia after she left home, and in it were lace curtains for the parlor windows. For her father there was a letter, which he read once and promptly burned in the kitchen stove. "She's all right," was all Sam would say to the girls. "She sends her love." It was the last of it she ever sent.

Even though the curtains made the parlor look grand, Arminda hated them. To her eyes, their finely wrought pattern was all sorrow and secrets. Twice a year, like punishment, they had to be taken down and washed, then attached with great care to a frame that kept them from shrinking as they dried. It was a horrid task, Min thought. The edges of the frame had hundreds of tiny sharp metal points to hold the loops of lace and pierce clumsy fingertips. She and Lucy worked with a rag between them to stop their own blood before it stained the clean curtains.

The terrible stretcher itself had to be borrowed before they could begin. Lucy always sent Min to get it from the Widow Dutton, half a mile beyond the bridge. Spring or fall, it seemed to Min that the wind never failed to blow raw when she made the trip. Nor could she escape Mrs. Dutton's demand for her to "set a spell" and listen to the exploits of her four married daughters and her bachelor son, who ran the farm. Sometimes Min feigned a cough and covered her mouth politely with a handkerchief when the old woman talked about her son, Leo. Min knew he wore his barnyard boots everywhere except to church. Besides, he had such a huge Adam's apple in his long unsightly neck that all the girls in Jericho laughed at him. Having to nod and smile while his mother talked about him was another price to be paid for Delia's curtains.

Early in the curtains' second spring, there was unexpected good weather, so warm and sunny that Lucy decreed Min should set up the stretcher outdoors. She chose an open spot along the run, where the low willows were just showing green. Stay away, birds, she thought grimly. Across the long field in the schoolyard, children screeched and shouted in celebration of noon recess. She wished she could still be one of them. Girls had no need of going on to school, her father said. His girls could read and figure with the best of them, and write a decent letter. Anything after that was too fancy. Anyway, there was plenty to do at home. Min sighed. She was too old for child's play, too young for courting, tired to death of housework. Sometimes she felt like an animal in a trap, with no voice to call, Let me out! Let me out!

"Arminda," Lucy said firmly, "you watch what you're doing! If you let this curtain drag on the ground, I'm not going to be the one that washes it over again." Lucy draped one end of the damp lace across her blue sleeve and swept her arm up and out. "Just look at it, Min. Isn't it beautiful? What would Edgar think if I had a dress like this?"

Min sniffed. "He'd think you were wearing a curtain."

"Honestly, Min! You may have your monthlies, but you're still just a child. Don't you ever think about boys—men—at all?"

Min felt a flush creep up her neck and into her cheeks. She thought plenty, if Lucy only knew it.

Her sister tossed her head, laughing. Sun gleamed on the fair hair that she always did up in a pouf, as if washday and Sunday were all the same to her. "Oh, Min," she said, "just look at you blush!"

Min turned away, pretending to steady the curtain frame, and stopped in midmotion. A horse and buggy stood at the edge of the road, and a woman in city clothes was picking her way through the wet grass.

"Be still!" Min whispered. "Someone's coming."

"Good afternoon, girls," the stranger called, and Min was immediately drawn to the lilt of her voice. Lucy dropped the curtain back into the wash basket and straightened her skirt.

"Would you be able to tell me if this is where Delia Walters lives?" The woman's eyes were green as moss on a stone. Min stared.

Lucy stepped forward. "Our sister has removed to the state of California," she said formally.

"Oh, my!" The woman touched her cheek with a tiny gloved hand. "I'm Mrs. Shannon—from the New Liberty Hotel, you know. I had no idea your sister had gone so far. I drove out to see if she could come back to work for us. She was so good, and we need someone so much just now."

Min thought that Mrs. Shannon was beautiful. The woman's dress was fawn colored, trimmed with dark braid and gold buttons that glittered in the sun. Min was dazzled.

"I just don't know what I'll do," Mrs. Shannon said. "Delia was the last good hope on my list."

Arminda stepped in front of her sister. "I'll come work for you," she said eagerly. "I'm good in the kitchen, and I can do just about any kind of housework." She gestured toward the basket at Lucy's feet. "I even know how to do up lace curtains. You have a lot of them at the hotel, I'll bet."

"Well, yes, we do. . . ." Mrs. Shannon looked surprised, but there was interest, too, in the way she set her lips and paused to think.

Say yes. Say yes. Take me, willed Min, being careful not to blink.

Lucy came forward then and put her arm lightly around Min's shoulders. "My little sister is only fourteen," she said. "I don't think our father or our brother Will would want her going off to work so young." She smiled. "They might allow me to do it, though."

The visitor ignored the pain on Min's face and turned to Lucy. "All right, then," she said brightly. "You're pretty enough to work in the dining room. Ask your father, and if everything's all right, come to us on Friday. You can room with one of our other girls at Mrs. Sardo's and come home on your days off the way Delia used to do."

When the arrangements were made and Mrs. Shannon had driven off in her buggy, when Lucy was bubbling with talk about how Min knew she was right and how wonderful it would be to live in town, then Min picked up the wash basket full of damp curtains and turned it upside down in the mud along the edge of the run. "If the hotel has so many curtains," she said, "I guess you'll need a lot of practice."

Arminda stalked off and was gone for hours, walking the roads and lanes that all led back to Jericho. She missed supper and came home with her apron pocket full of wildflowers. Will threatened her with the razor strap, big as she was, because Lucy was distraught and Delia's curtains were all but ruined. Good, thought Min. She and Lucy barely spoke for weeks afterward, and still it was a long time before she could find it in her heart to be sorry.

9

THE BACK PORCH STEPS at Gram and Grandpa's house are concrete, rough and still warm against Angela's legs as she sits in the fading light. She is here to claim private space, to put distance between herself and the family laboring in the kitchen, trying to talk things out.

"This might take longer to heal than if you'd broken it—you know that, don't you?"

"Well, I just refuse to be a nuisance. A couple more of these pills and I'll be up and around in no time. Tomorrow, maybe."

"You can't rush it too much, though, Katherine. Do you think Virginia could come over and help out?"

Someone laughs. "With that ornery little boy?"

"What's for sure is that you kids need to get on back home and get your own work done."

Angela can see them all without looking—

Grandpa still in his fishing vest, Dad at the table with a cup of coffee that he isn't drinking. Her mother has cleared up the mess of their takeout dinner, brought from New Liberty on her trip home from the emergency room with Gram. Gram is sitting in a soft chair from the living room, her injured leg wrapped like a mummy and propped on a stool. GrandMin's wheelchair sits in the doorway between the dining room and kitchen. Brian has given her a lapful of papers and packets from one of the attic cartons that Angela carried from the old house. To keep Min's mind off things, is how he has explained it, but Angela is sure that Gram wanted to sort through those boxes herself first.

Angela can hear their voices clearly; she is confident that she will not miss more than a word or two, should she choose to listen. But she has thinking to do, private things of her own to sort out. Already she knows that one decision is final. She and her mother will stay on at Gram's, although no one is saying for how long.

"I told you, Pop, Angie and I are staying." In the kitchen Carol is repeating it even now. "Don't argue."

Angela sighs and smacks at a few of the mosquitoes that have gathered to keep her company. The person she most wants to talk to now is Tessa. She wants to know if it will be okay, if her friends at home will all have other friends by the time she gets back. She wants to know if she and Tessa will still have things to talk about when school starts. She considers this other life of hers, the one where seventh grade waits, where Tessa helps her figure how she's going to fit. It isn't perfect, she knows that, but it's her own life and she likes it. She misses it.

Angela takes a deep breath and fills her nose with the perfume of Gram's old-fashioned roses, growing like tiny pink cabbages on a bush that droops over the edge of the steps. A day ago the thought of staying here beyond Sunday would have sent her into a rage of weeping. Now she is only melancholy. The difference, she tells herself, is that now, with Gram hurt, she is really needed here. No one will be making up things for her to do. The other difference—she thinks of Tessa and can't help smiling—is Tom.

Angela pictures him in small parts: hair, sweatband, soiled shirt, ice gray eyes. As always, her attempts to think reasonably about Tom Ferris turn into feelings rather than words, something that operates by pulse beat, not brain power. It makes her feel giddy and a little embarrassed, and she hopes that Tessa can explain it to her.

Behind her, Brian pushes his nose against the kitchen screen. "Hsst, Angie! Look up here, you buffalo."

"Go away." She feels like a sleeper, wakened too fast.

"You'll be sorry."

She looks up warily.

"Mom says go around front and see what Tom lover-boy wants. He just rode up on that thing he calls a bicycle."

Angela makes herself get up slowly in spite of a suddenly lurching heart. "You're such a pain," she says, but Brian slips easily out of her mind as she rounds the corner of the house.

Tom lets his bike fall in the grass and walks up the driveway toward her, carrying something wrapped in a towel. He smiles when he sees her.

"My mother made you guys some cinnamon rolls," he says. "For breakfast, I guess. She thinks your grandmother has had a pretty hard time, even before this."

With both hands Angela takes the pan, still warm through the cloth that covers it. "That was nice of her. Thanks." She wants to say something special, but only ordinary words come. "I . . . like cinnamon rolls."

Tom is standing very close to her. His chin is above the top of her head; he is taller than she thought.

"Are you gonna be all right?" His voice is too quiet now for anyone inside to hear. "You seemed all shaky this afternoon."

Caught unprepared for kindness, Angela hopes she is not going to cry. In all today's uproar, no one else has thought to ask how *she* is feeling.

"I'm okay," she says, thinking she should take just one little step back, although her feet seem to be planted here at the edge of the driveway. She feels that if she does not move, he will surely touch her and then she won't know what to do. Please! she says to herself, but she is not sure if that means please do or please don't.

"You staying?"

"For a while." She can't see his face clearly without tipping her head back, and for some reason she is afraid to do that.

"Good," he says. "I'll see you around, then." She feels his breath as he dips his head and touches his face against her hair. Was it his lips? Could it have been accidental?

He is away and gone without another word, clattering out to the road on his rickety bicycle.

Angela moves slowly toward the house, burdened by sweet confusion, overwhelmed by a feeling she cannot name, older in an instant. Shakespeare's heroines are suddenly within her reach.

"Angie! Where are you?" Her father's voice rings out impatiently in the dark, and she begins to hurry.

Brian waits at the kitchen door to take the pan she has almost forgotten she is carrying. "Did you have a good nuzzle?" he whispers.

Angela ignores him. She blinks, trying to shed one life for another, night vision for the brightness of the room. Her eyes rest for a moment on GrandMin and then fasten there in surprise. Min is sitting still as a stump among fallen leaves, old pictures strewn on the floor around her. Some lie flat, some crumpled. A few are torn.

"Why, Mother!" Gram says, following Angela's gaze. "Whatever possessed you?"

———

Arminda had cooked and cleaned for Blossom Clark more than a year, and gladly, because without Mrs. Clark she would still have been home every day of every week, buried away at sixteen with no one but Pa and his rocker for company. Lucy had become a regular town girl, taking buggy rides with suitors on her days off and seldom getting home. Will had his own house and a wife to take care of it—Ermabeth Frazey's sister Lillian, who wasn't as pretty as Ermabeth and only half as righteous. Wheat was gone, too, living in Denver with Jesse and working at things that might possibly make him rich but probably wouldn't. The two of them took infrequent turns sending picture postcards with grand signatures but no message.

Sam Walters kept his youngest child close as an egg in a nest. Min had given up asking to go anywhere or do anything except for church meetings and taking the mending basket to her friend Carrie Allison's front porch. Then old Mrs. Clark, who lived alone, imprisoned by rheumatism and her own eccentricities, sent word around Jericho that she needed to hire a girl for housework. Arminda didn't give one eye-blink of attention. But then her father said, "Poor Blossom. Poor thing. She and Molly were real close, years ago." And he sent Arminda, astonished and eager, to work for Mrs. Clark and scrub the biggest house in town.

Within a week Min loved her employer, who had a kind heart and a gift for telling stories. Many were about the mother that Arminda could no longer remember, and these she took home at night to her pa, a treat for the late supper they shared in the house empty but for the two of them.

Blossom Clark was a childless widow, but she had nephews in abundance. Long before Arminda met any of them, she admired them in a photograph that hung in a place of honor on Mrs. Clark's front-parlor wall. It was a picture of ten young men at a picnic ground, all of them handsome. Min fancied a tall boyish one who leaned against a tree. One morning when she had finished baking and was getting out the rags to dust, she could stand it no longer. She lifted the picture down and carried it, heavy frame and all, to the chair lined with pillows where Blossom Clark spent her days.

"Who is this?" Min demanded.

"Why, those are all of Mr. Clark's brothers' boys." Blossom's small cheerful mouth was underscored by ample chins, which lay in crescents like extra smiles all the way down to her bosom. "The one you're pointing to is Firman, Alexander's youngest. He must be twenty by now, I suppose. And we'll see a lot of him this year, in the flesh, don't you know, because he'll be going back and forth to work at Edgar Elliot's store in New Liberty, coming right this way, and he's promised to stop and I don't know what-all his mother wrote me, and . . ." Her voice trailed off, the way it often did.

A small spot of color rose in each of Min's cheeks.

"Mind you don't break the glass when you hang that back up," Blossom said kindly to her silence.

It was barely April, rainy and gray, when Firman Clark made his first visit with Aunt Blossom. No one had announced his coming, so there was not much more than cold beef and biscuits for Arminda to lay out for lunch. She was in the middle of the first of spring cleaning, anyway, washing down the walls in the back bedroom, a job that left her bedraggled and irritable. It was too busy a time to be sociable, even if Firman had been a friendly sort, which he didn't seem to be. He nodded at her once when introduced and turned back immediately to his auntie. Min studied his profile and his dark, dark hair and thought it was a waste of a good face for him to be so high and mighty.

When the weather improved, Firman made another visit, and if Blossom knew he was coming she didn't tell. The apple trees were blooming then, and Min was gathering clothes off the line when his horse and buggy clopped in by the shed. "Miss Arminda!" he called in greeting, and showed her a smile worthy of his face. She was surprised that he remembered her name and glad that Mrs. Clark invited her to sit and help drink the tea Min had made for them. Young Firman told witty stories about all his cousins, and he talked easily about big plans.

"I'm saving to buy an automobile," he said, "but they aren't easy to get, you know, so I might have to build one myself."

Bragger, Min thought, but she smiled and was impressed in spite of herself.

In June he came again, twice, and by July it was once a week.

"Your nephew must think the world of you, Mrs. Clark," Arminda called one afternoon as she rolled and cut the dough for sugar cakes made with sour cream. She had put by four lemons for lemonade, too; Firman had complimented her on it the last time. "He's so good to visit, don't you think?"

Blossom's laugh started as a chuckle and came rolling up out of her. "Come in here to me, child," she directed. When Arminda appeared, the old woman handed up the mirror she used for plucking chin whiskers. "Look in there, dear girl," she said, "and tell me who that young man comes to see."

The face Min saw blazed pink as peonies, with clear eyes under straight brows. "Well . . ." she said.

"I don't cook," Blossom said, "and I don't look like the first breath of spring either. But I'm a pretty good matchmaker if I do say so myself."

Min was speechless. It was not that she didn't know, hadn't known. It was just that all of a sudden she had a name for her condition: happiness.

10

IT IS TUESDAY, and GrandMin does not want to be taken care of now. If she can't have Katy, she doesn't want anyone. The ankle is making slow progress; once a day up and down the stairs is all the activity Gram can manage. Angela sees the frustration in her grandmother's face when Min calls for her, "Kate? Katy? Can you come here a minute?" And of course Gram can't.

When the two women sit in the same room, Gram has to reassure GrandMin over and over that someone is taking care of her, of both of them.

"Have they left you all alone?" Min asks. "Have they all left us?"

"No, Mother, of course not. We're getting along fine," Gram says, now one way, now another. "We're fine here watching the news. That's President Reagan talking, did you see?" Or, "We're fine, Mother. Willard Scott says it's going to be hot." Angela thinks her own head will explode.

On Sunday when Dad left for home, she celebrated in silence that Brian was with him. Now she is beginning to be glad that they are coming back for the weekend. It is a relief not to be teased, but at least Brian is someone young. She is tired of being always with adults—old, older, oldest. Her thoughts touch Tom Ferris, as they have countless times in the past four days. But she hasn't seen Tom, and she wouldn't have time to go looking for him if she dared.

Angela is dismayed to be so busy, now that she is trying to do part of Gram's work. Her mother does the most, almost running, it seems, between Gram's kitchen and the old house with its half-finished wallpaper. There are breakfast trays, lunch trays, laundry, dishes. The dishes have no end. Why doesn't Gram have a dishwasher? she thinks. How does—did—Gram do it all? When Angela thinks about life and what she will do someday, the picture is never cluttered like this with housework.

By Wednesday Min asks to stay in bed. "I believe I won't get up today," she whispers when Angela goes into the bedroom to open her blinds for the morning.

"You'll have to sit up for your tea, won't you, GrandMin? And to eat? You can't have breakfast lying flat like that."

Min seems not to hear. She raises one hand off

her cotton coverlet and extends all four crooked fingers in Angela's direction. The thumb stays bent against her palm. "Are you the same girl that has the pretty hair?" she says.

Angela touches her ponytail self-consciously, but she is teaching herself to ignore questions like this. "It's going to be 95 degrees today, GrandMin," she says, to change the subject. "I heard the weather on TV." Gram has already directed Carol to close the doors and windows against the heat to come.

"No," Min says. "It's cool today, just like yesterday."

"But we've been having a heat wave!"

A sigh spirals up and hangs above the pillow. "Find me another cover, will you, girl?"

"Angela." She says her own name slowly so that maybe, this time, the old woman will remember it. She studies her great-grandmother's face and wonders if she is really getting thinner, if her eyes have always been set so deep. "I don't know where the extra covers are, GrandMin. I'll have to go ask."

In the kitchen Gram's chair and stool are pushed close to the table, where she and Carol are finishing mugs of tea.

"She says she's cold, Mom," Angela reports. "She wants another cover."

"On a day like today?"

Gram smooths one of the crumpled pictures she is sorting and taps it with her finger, absently. "It's her circulation, Angel. It doesn't work any better than the rest of her anymore. Did she get her pills this morning?"

"Not yet." Angela looks down without interest at the photograph's distorted faces. "She won't even sit up to drink her tea, Gram. She wants to stay in bed."

"You see?" Gram looks at Carol. "I ought to be up taking care of her."

"Now, Mother—"

"Should I get her a blanket or something?" Angela persists, but the other two are no longer listening.

"What we ought to do," Carol says, "is call that doctor who promised to come out here if you needed him."

"We'll never get him to come, you know that. But I suppose he might give us some advice."

"She's failing, Mom. We all can see it."

"Oh, I know," says Gram. "I know." Such a stillness comes over her grandmother that Angela has to turn away. If she watches, thinks what Gram could be thinking, it will make her cry.

"I'll just get the afghan off the couch for her," she announces into the silence. "And then . . ." her eyes flick to the clock over the stove, "then

I'll go get the mail for you, Gram, before it gets too hot." She needs to be outside, with more air to breathe and less to think about.

On the way to the post office, immediately lighter in spirit, she concentrates on Tom. Maybe he is out this morning, too. She imagines him everywhere, watching for her, waiting. She knows how unlikely this is, but the images come to her anyway, unbidden. The post office, which she reaches without having seen even one person, is a little brick building with bright petunias and two flags in front. Inside, Mrs. Melvin smiles from behind the wire grille where she dispenses stamps and money orders.

"How are the shut-ins today?" she asks.

"About the same, I guess." Angela takes the slim stack of mail for her grandparents with a smile. She likes Mrs. Melvin and her big dangly earrings, every day a different pair. Even so, she doesn't feel like going into details about GrandMin. What could she say?

"You tell your grandmother I'm going to stop by this evening, you hear? I've got a few late strawberries, and I want her to have them."

"She'll like that," Angela says politely, beginning to edge backward. She might still run into Tom, she thinks.

"And honey," Mrs. Melvin goes on, "you're going to have to meet my niece, Cherie. She's visiting this week. You're just about the same age, you two—or maybe she's a bit older, I don't know. She was just in here a minute ago with her can of pop. Shoot, I can't get her to eat right. Every time she comes, I want her to have a good breakfast, but no, she's out and gone, looking for someone to talk to. What a girl."

Angela smiles again, halfway. It is always such a risky thing to meet someone new that she dreads it—unlike Tessa, who seems to live for the sight of an unfamiliar face. Yet this Cherie person might be someone she could talk to, someone to help her get through the days.

"She just walked on down by the bridge, I think," Mrs. Melvin says. "You could go down that way and say hello right now."

"Maybe I will," Angela calls on her way out. "Thanks!" She hurries; she thinks she remembers that the Ferrises live somewhere near the bridge. Anyway, it will be better than going back to Gram's this very minute.

From the post office to Willow Creek, the road is shaded, but shimmering hot. Her clothing begins to stick to her skin as she moves. She pulls at the tank top clinging to her middle, wishing she had worn her blue big shirt today, the gauzy one. If she does happen to see Tom, she wants to look okay, not all fussy and rumpled and stupid. In the yard she is passing, two little boys chasing each other with water guns try to use her for a target, and she has to run.

At the edge of the bridge she stops to rest. No one seems to be around. She is thinking that she has used all this extra energy for nothing when her eye catches on something red that flashes through the green undergrowth of the bank below. A giggle bounces along the water, and two figures appear, a girl in red shorts holding a can of pop and a boy with no shirt. Tom. Angela watches, waiting to breathe.

The girl puts her pop can on a rock and throws something that splashes heavily into the water. She giggles again, a high sound that covers whatever Tom is saying. Now he picks up a stone and hands it to the girl, and now he stands behind her, close, and stretches his right arm along hers, grasping the back of her hand. Their two arms, as one, sweep back to the side in a wide arc and snap forward so that the stone from her hand skips neatly along the surface of the water— once, twice, three times, four—and then sinks.

"Perfect!" squeals the girl. She turns and puts her arms around Tom Ferris as if she does it every day. And then he bends down a little bit and kisses her, as if that isn't a new thing either.

The huge breath Angela has been holding seeps away like air from yesterday's balloon. She steps backward and turns without looking, with no thought for traffic. She walks fast, almost runs. Her eyes are on her feet, her hands clenched on Grandpa's mail, her mind fastened on escape. All she knows now is that she wants to be away from here, from Gatesville, from Gram's, from everything. The only place she wants to be now is home.

———

Winter came early to Jericho the year that Arminda kept company with Firman Clark. On the first of November, when he came to sit with her on his Aunt Blossom's front porch, he took off his coat and rolled up his shirt-sleeves, it was that warm. But before Thanksgiving, there was a blizzard and a foot of snow that stayed and stayed. Min didn't care. It made the town dazzling by sunlight, blue-white and beautiful under the moon. She ignored the cold beneath her feet and gave thanks for the sturdy runners on Firman's sleigh, which brought him to her almost as often as his summer buggy.

"Look at that, how everything glitters," Blossom Clark said, enjoying the view from her window. "Just like it's been decorated. We should have a party. Next time Firman comes, we should have a party." The idea attached itself and grew until Blossom seemed to think of nothing else. The neighbors would be invited, and Firman's mama, though she might not want to make the trip in the cold, and Arminda's father, and Lucy, if she could have a day off, and Will and his wife, if those two could unbend far enough to have a good time. Blossom warmed so to her topic that she took to wrapping herself in only three shawls instead of four. They would welcome the Chirstmas season with plates of food and a taffy pull and sleigh rides and songs. And then, if the preacher went home early enough, they would pull back the parlor furniture, wind up the phonograph, and dance.

Min was agog. She had been to church suppers and community sings and once to a real party at Carrie Allison's house, but she had never had a hand in planning such an event. From the beginning she guessed it would be a lot of work, and it was. Blossom insisted on writing the invitations in her own spidery scrawl, but it was Min who walked them to the post office, Min who cleaned, Min who baked, Min who went up to the store in a bitter wind to get an extra package of powdered cloves. It was Min who went home so tired at night she could scarcely lift the skillet to get supper for her pa.

"If it wasn't for those shiny eyes of yours," Sam Walters said, "I'd have to think you work too hard over at Blossom's."

"Oh, no," protested Arminda. "No, it's fun." But she did wonder if she could keep going.

Then the great day arrived, cold but clear, and everything seemed to be done. Mrs. Clark's kitchen floor was as clean as it was going to get, the bread was out of the oven and the ham was in, the potatoes were peeled, two kinds of pie and one huge cake were waiting in the pantry. Before Min went home to pretty up, Blossom stopped her.

"What have we forgotten, Arminda?"

"Nothing, I hope." She was too excited to notice how much her arms ached from all her work.

"Are you going to wear that green bow in your hair to match your dress?"

Min blushed. "If you think it isn't too fancy." It was something of Delia's that she had found in the back of a drawer and brought one day for Blossom's opinion.

"It's a party, child," the old woman said, almost reproachfully. "Let's see you smile."

Min smiled.

"Now let's see you dance a step or two."

There was a small silence. "I can't," Min said finally. "I don't know how." As little girls, she and Lucy had danced together once or twice in the kitchen at home, but Will had caught them at it and raised such a ruckus they had never tried again. Will said that dancing led to the devil's work. Min didn't believe that, but at the time, with Will talking about his razor strap, it had just been easier not to argue.

Blossom shook her head. "You'll have to dance," she said. "Firman loves to dance. All the Clark boys do. They're foolish over it."

"Can you teach—?" Min began a question and bit it off. Mrs. Clark was a slave to gravity now, surely no dancing instructor. It was unfair even to ask.

But Blossom's face was alight. "I was a dancing fool myself once," she said. "Go get the broom!" She sang and sang in her wheezy voice while Arminda clutched her skinny dance partner and struggled to follow the directions Blossom gave with her hands. After a time Min's body found its own rhythm, and she floated back and forth in a graceful zigzag pattern up and down the room.

"You've got it!" Blossom cried. "You're waltzing!" She sighed with satisfaction as Min and the broom whirled to a stop. "Your mother would be so proud, " she said softly, and Min had to turn away and bite her lip.

"Go on now," Blossom directed. "Look in on the ham once and then go home and get yourself ready. They'll be here before you know it."

———

The party itself was everything Min had hoped, and more. Blossom had never said that the neighbors might bring more food, or that some of the women might take over the kitchen and shoo her away to have fun with the other young people. Min reveled in her freedom and in having Firman by her side. He said that the green bow was very becoming to her, and he bragged on her cooking and was charming as could be when he talked to her father. He tucked her into the sleigh right beside him when they went out on the snow. Lucy and a friend of hers and Leo Dutton and the youngest Allison boy all piled into the back. They whooped and sang as far as the schoolhouse, where they got out and threw snowballs just like children—even Leo— and then whooped and sang some more on the way back.

Mrs. Otterby had organized the taffy pull so that when the sleigh riders unbundled themselves there was just time for them to rub their hands with butter and get started. They paired off to claim shares of the sugary mixture that would become shiny and stiff with enough stretching. Everyone laughed at Homer Gates, the postmaster, who didn't get enough butter on his hands and had candy stuck to every finger.

"Looks like you got a handful of lollipops, Homer!"

"Stay away from dogs and little kids, Homer!"

It was a wonderful party. They ate, and played forfeits, and ate again, and laughed and sang. Blossom Clark was like the director of a giant, noisy band, pointing here and there to get things started or keep them going. Will and Lillian came by at suppertime for ham and pie, but left early along with the Reverend Mr. Langley. After that there was dancing, and for Min, things began to blur. Afterward she remembered that Firman held her as close as she thought he dared while they waltzed, and he whispered that she was a feather in his arms. She remembered that someone else, maybe Johnny Allison, had stepped all over her feet and that Leo Dutton had asked her to dance but she had been smart enough to say she was too tired.

Long after midnight, when she lay exhausted but sleepless in her own bed, she remembered the warmth and the music and the voices. The party played over and over in her head like the rolls on Mrs. Clark's phonograph, in good rhythm at first, slowing as time wore on. Firman whirled behind her eyes, his face, his high collar, his hand on her back as they waltzed. Around and around the heady music played, but with a snag, a scratch in the record cylinder that kept her from sleep. Suddenly Min sat up. She knew what it was. She remembered. She remembered seeing guests to the door on Blossom Clark's behalf while the clock struck twelve, and in the parlor music still played and someone still danced. Two someones danced and spoke low, one face close to the other. All that long time Min had stood and said, "Good-bye." "Thank you for coming." "Yes, wasn't Mrs. Clark clever to think of it?" "Good night, I'll see you in church." All that long time Firman had danced with her sister Lucy.

Firman had danced with Lucy. What was the harm in that? Arminda thought she knew, and the knowing made her weep into her pillow.

11

"THIS IS UNCLE WILL, I think," Angela's grandmother says, squinting at one of the faded photographs arranged in her hand like playing cards. "I don't know who that is with him. It's too tall for Aunt Lillian. Here, Angel, write his name on the back the way I showed you—without pressing down so it won't show through."

Angela puts out her hand for the picture and tries to concentrate. She knows it will be better for her if she thinks about what she is doing rather than about what happened at the bridge this morning, yet her mind keeps turning that over and over the same way her stomach is tumbling her lunch.

"What did you say his name was?" She has unfastened her hair, which lies hot against her neck.

Gram looks at her sharply, and for a moment Angela thinks she will say, "Pay attention!" like Miss Rogers in last year's science class. But

Gram's eyes soften and the voice she uses is her patient one.

"William Walters. My uncle Will. He was GrandMin's brother, the next to oldest one."

Angela holds the picture in both hands, pretending to study it.

"I'll bet you wanted to go to the mall in New Liberty with your mom," Gram says unexpectedly. "I do hate to have us be such a bother, Angel, but I'm just not up to dealing with an emergency by myself if Mother should have one."

Poor Gram, Angela thinks. Her own hurt dwindles just enough to make room for a little sympathy. She gets up, pads barefoot to her grandmother's chair, and gives her a one-armed hug. "You're not a bother," she says. "You could never be."

"Oh, Angel." Gram's voice goes flat. "We all get on in years. It comes to all of us."

Angela squeezes her grandmother's shoulder once more, almost too hard. "No," she says, "you're special." And Angela means it. She cannot, will not, think of Gram in GrandMin's place. "You'll get older, Gram," she says, "but it won't matter."

Gram's smile is narrow and wry. "Silly child," she says fondly.

Relieved, Angela smiles back and returns to

her place at the cluttered dining room table. She waggles Uncle Will's picture to draw Gram's attention back to it. "This person really looks fierce," she says.

"Well, he was, at least when I knew him. Mean-spirited and stingy both, that's what your GrandMin always said. He lost all that hair and got bald as an egg, but he grew a beard long enough to make up for it. I was scared to death of him when I was a little girl. He and his family moved away, like all the rest." She shakes her head. "They only come back to be buried."

Angela shuffles through the stack of pictures still waiting for labels. "Who's this?" The man in the photograph sits stiffly on a couch, one arm curved around a very small boy.

"I'm not sure. It could be Grandpa Walters, I suppose, when he was younger. And that could be any one of Min's brothers, or some little neighbor, or anyone. Who knows?" Gram makes a face. "This is so frustrating, Angel. Here are all these pictures that I don't remember ever seeing before—they must have been up in that attic for sixty or seventy years. Mother can't say beans about them now, and I can't make head or tail out of most of them. But this one does look like Grandpa must have looked before his hair went white. He was such a dear old soul."

"You had me take flowers to his grave, right?"

Angela asks. The question brings that day in the cemetery back to her so strong and fresh that it takes real effort not to be distracted. "Oh," she says, flipping fast from one picture to another. "Here's a pretty girl. Do you know who she is?"

"Goodness," Gram says. "Give me time."

Angela points. "Look at those dreamy eyes." It occurs to her that Tessa gets this look sometimes. She has always admired it, but no matter how long she stands at the mirror, she cannot duplicate it.

"I think I do know who this is," Gram says. "It's Aunt Lucy. Must be. It's the dress I recognize, though, not the face. She got married in this dress and then when she finally had Helen after all those boys, she cut it up and made Helen a little shift. Helen wore it until it was nothing but a rag, and every time she came to visit she'd stick her nose in the air and say, 'Look at me, look at me.' " Gram laughs. "That Helen was a corker, just like Aunt Lucy. Maybe Mother would recognize this one. Sneak in with it, will you, Angel, and see if she's awake. I'd love to know if this really is Lucy in her wedding dress."

Angela sighs. "She won't know, will she?" She dreads going into GrandMin's room.

"Try her anyway. I'd keep this picture in one of our albums if it was really Lucy. She and Mother were close when they were girls."

Angela's reluctant bare feet go soundlessly across the hall and into Min's room. "GrandMin?"

"Is that you, Delia?" The old woman's voice seems higher than usual, and a little thick.

A nameless tingle chases itself up and down Angela's back. "It's me, GrandMin. Angela. I've got a picture Gram wants you to look at."

"Oh. Did Katy have her picture taken?" Min's words are suddenly clearer.

"No, GrandMin. She wants you to look at this one." With one hand Angela props the old portrait on Min's chest; with the other she loops the earpieces of Min's glasses gingerly in place. "There," she says. "Do you know who that is?"

Min frowns and takes two ragged little breaths like hiccups. Then she pushes the picture away.

"Don't you know this person?" Angela asks again, feeling a little smug. She knew it was useless to try. She reaches to get the picture, hair swinging down on both sides of her face. Suddenly GrandMin's hand comes up and tangles itself in Angela's curls. Angela gasps.

"Come here," Min says urgently, pulling. "Come here."

"Ouch, GrandMin, don't! You're hurting me!" Angela tries to shake her head free, but Min is holding tight.

"Don't go," Min pleads. "Stay with me." Deep

behind her polished lenses, the eyes she fastens on Angela are huge and murky. The old woman's breath fills up Angela's nose. "Help me get back to Jericho," she whispers. "I don't know what they've done with it. Please!" Her hand pulls Angela close, and Angela screams.

———

That evening, when Virginia comes to visit with Carol and her mother at the kitchen table, Angela keeps her distance, but she is aware of every word. Grandpa has taken Garth by the hand and disappeared with him into the garden; nothing covers the kitchen voices, low as they are.

"I had to limp in there myself and make Mother let go of her," Gram says. "The poor child. I don't know what's next."

"Of all the times for me to get in a slow check-out line at the grocery," complains Angela's mother. "If I'd only been here."

Virginia's voice is young and certain. "It's her medicine. She needs to have it adjusted or something."

"Well," Carol says, "the doctor promised to come Saturday, thank goodness. But when I ran through all her symptoms for him, he said he didn't think there would be any reason to put her in the hospital."

"But maybe when he sees her . . ." Gram lets her words trail off.

"If she was *my* old grandma," Virginia says, "I surefire know what I would do."

Near midnight, when the late news is over and Angela is wondering how she will get to sleep, her mother comes and sits on the arm of the couch, sharing in the weak breeze from the fan.

"We'll talk to the doctor about GrandMin," her mother says abruptly. "Gram agrees we'll probably have to do something about temporary care, at least. Then you and I can go home, I guess. Gram can manage if she only has herself to look after."

"Home?" Unprepared, Angela feels that she has swallowed too much air. "Really?"

Her mother smiles and runs one finger under a damp curl that has escaped Angela's stretchy hairband. "We need to be home, don't we?" She sounds rueful.

Angela sits up cross-legged and cools herself by fanning the loose middle of her pajamas. "So is Virginia coming to help?"

Carol rolls her eyes. "Hardly."

"You're going to hire a nurse?"

"Angie, you know we don't have that kind of money. Think what it would cost to hire for three shifts, or even two."

"I don't know," Angela says truthfully. She has no idea. In truth, she doesn't care. She is going home.

"It'll have to be a nursing home, Angie. I just hope that ValleyCare place has an opening." Her mother frowns. "I thought it was all right, didn't you? Clean and everything, I mean."

"Oh," Angela says. She does want to go home. She needs to be with her friends, with Tessa, away from here. "I remember that place," she says, and feels cold enough now without fanning.

———

The second Sunday in September, Firman Clark and Lucy Walters stood up in his aunt Blossom's parlor, because it was big enough for all the family, and got married. Arminda had a throbbing headache and wanted to stay home, but her pa wouldn't let her. "Now's the time to show your spunk," he said to her in private as he patted her shoulder.

Lucy wanted Min to help her get her hair just right. "Please don't mope around and ruin my wedding day, Min," she said. "It's not like you were promised to Firman or anything like that." No, thought Min, nothing like that.

As soon as the ceremony was over, Min slipped out and walked the mile from Blossom's house to the cemetery. It was unseasonably cool, and she shivered in the good gray dress she had worn to church all summer.

"Hello, Mama," she said out loud, and propped herself against the stone that marked her mother's grave. It was a place to think, and what she thought was how much she would miss Blossom Clark, now that Lucy and Firman were going to live with her and take care of the place in exchange for inheriting it someday. Blossom would miss her, too, she was sure of it.

"I think Firman's making a mistake," Mrs. Clark had confided to Min one day, "but I comfort myself with the thought that at least it's another of Molly's girls."

If only Molly were still here to help sort things out, Min thought, rubbing her mother's stone.

Her reverie was shattered by a voice, a loud and rasping voice that called, "Arminda! Arminda, I've brought you a coat!"

"I don't want a coat!" Arminda shouted back. Who did Leo Dutton think he was, following her around like a broody hen after a chick? For months he had kept her in his sights, offered her wagon rides when she didn't need to go anywhere and seats at church meetings when she'd rather stand. It was a wonder he'd gotten any of his farm work done.

"Please leave me alone," Min said in her fiercest voice as his bony frame cast its gaunt shadow over her.

"You need a coat," he insisted.

Min stared at her own hands in her lap rather than look at him. She was sure he was the ugliest man in Jericho—nothing but neck and then that little bald spot he was getting. He was thirty if he was a day.

"Just go away," said Min, but he didn't. He was bound to talk to her and then walk her home.

Months later, looking back, she saw that Leo had simply worn her down with his presence. He was always there, somewhere—dropping by to talk to Pa, bringing in some of the cider he had pressed, hovering at church. He was a little better looking when he smiled, but that wasn't often. She discovered that he could sing and whistle well enough to deceive the birds. Now and then he said something that made her laugh.

Leo became such a natural part of things that when he said, "You'll marry me, won't you, Arminda?" she said, "Yes" without thinking, as if she were agreeing to some meaningless comment about the weather. Her father thought it was a satisfactory arrangement; Leo had land to farm, so the couple wouldn't want for a living. As for Min, she thought she might as well be doing dishes in a kitchen she could think of as her own. Feelings didn't really enter into it. Love was for dreamy girls like Lucy anyway. Min harbored a secret guilty pleasure in knowing that love had already brought her sister many mornings of wretchedness along with her newly fat waist.

On a cold, dry day just before Christmas, Min and Leo went off by themselves to be married. Her nose was runny and red by the time his old slow horse had pulled the buggy to New Liberty. It was so late in the day that the preacher who was to marry them had his hat on, ready to leave for other important business; but he was persuaded to stay long enough to say the right words and sign the right papers.

"Best wishes, then, Mrs. Dutton," he said finally, clasping Min's hand, and she felt herself stiffen. The only Mrs. Dutton she knew was now her mother-in-law, the woman who had offered them curtain stretchers as a wedding gift. It felt odd, having the same name.

Leo took her to spend the night at the New Liberty Hotel, a glaring waste of money to Arminda's way of thinking, but exciting, too. He bought her a fine dinner in the very room where Lucy had carried so many fancy plates to fancy people. Later on, in the room assigned them on the second floor, there was a bad moment when

Min wished she knew more about being married. Why had she been too stubborn to let Lucy talk to her, the way Lucy wanted? Most of her information about men and women together came from Carrie Allison, who apparently didn't have it right. But that moment passed, and it surprised Min more than a little that she was glad to be with Leo, glad to be his new wife on a cold night in a comfortable bed.

In the morning they got their things together, claimed the horse and buggy from the barn behind the hotel, and set out for home, for Jericho. They had agreed to stay, for the time being, with Min's father, and she sat back in anticipation of seeing him, of telling him that she was happy. But Leo had one more stop to make.

"Step down here, Arminda," Leo said—he never in his life called her Min—"and come along." The storefront sign said SEBRING PHOTO-GRAPHS. "We're going to have your wedding picture taken."

New color rose behind the winter pink on Min's cold cheeks. "I don't need to have my picture taken just because Lucy did," she protested.

"It's nothing to do with Lucy," he said, taking her arm. "It's me that wants your picture."

"It'll be both of us, then," Min said. "A wedding picture should have two."

Leo shook his head. "I don't care to see my own picture," he said, and no amount of arguing would change his mind.

"But I'm not fixed up for a picture, Leo," she begged. "My collar's all rumply and my hair is every which way. And just look at this ribbon."

"Please," he said. "For me. I like the way you look."

And so, for his sake, she had her picture taken. "Don't blink," said the photographer, and then, just as he pressed the shutter, "Good, Mrs. Dutton, very good."

Later, when the photograph was in her hands, Min saw that her eyes had stayed open wide and clear, but her smile had faded completely. She seemed to stare at the camera with grim determination.

"You look like you could wrestle bears," Leo said approvingly, but Min was embarrassed and made him promise to hide that picture forever.

1 2

On Friday, the hottest of that week's hot, bright days, it seems to Angela that everyone's time is filled with waiting. Gram is sure that it will storm, she says, and from noon on she watches the sky at one window after another. In between glances she hobbles from counter to kitchen table and back, working on a pie for Brian and Jay, who are supposed to arrive for supper.

"Mom, you shouldn't be doing all this," Carol says. "You'll wear yourself out."

"I need to keep busy," Kate says. "I can't just sit forever." Angela notices that Gram winces whenever she takes a step. Brian doesn't need pie that bad, Angela thinks, but she doesn't say anything because somehow, today, Gram isn't easy to talk to.

Angela's mother waits for the phone. She has a note pad with businesslike headings all ready to take information about the nursing homes she has called. Four of the six have promised that someone will get back to her by tomorrow. Her mother is rubbing her forehead a lot, Angela notices, and running her fingers through her short hair so often that by midafternoon she has taken on a wild look.

"You should comb your hair, Mom," Angela says.

"Honestly!" snaps Carol, and goes right on folding laundry.

Angela is waiting, too—waiting to know when she can go home, waiting to know what will happen with GrandMin. Today no one has asked her to go in Min's room, not once. Her mother and her grandmother have made all the trips, carried all the dishes that are as full coming out as going in. Angela's day has been easier in a way, but uncomfortable, too, as if she is avoiding some unpleasant but necessary thing. She wishes that she could go in and sit down and talk to the old woman like a normal person.

Listen, GrandMin, she imagines herself saying, *I hated that nursing home and I hate to think of you in it, but you know that Gram can't take care of you now. Don't you see that? And that my mom and I can't stay here on and on? We have a home and friends and things to do, and . . .* Even in her head Angela cannot finish this speech. She wonders if it would be cruel to tell GrandMin that they are taking her to Jericho, if they do take her anywhere. Maybe, she thinks, this week will just go on repeating itself forever.

When Angela's grandfather comes home from work, even he seems less than patient for once. "Hotter than a pistol out there." He pours a drink from the squat blue pitcher that is always in the refrigerator. "That boy didn't come, did he?" He doesn't even plant a kiss on Gram's forehead, the way he usually does.

"Who?" she says.

"Oh, Tom what's-his-name. He promised to mow both these yards before it rained again, and I see he hasn't even started."

Angela swallows. One of the reasons she wants to go home is that she doesn't want to see Tom Ferris ever again in her life. Not that she wants to make extra work for Grandpa, but she hopes that Tom will forget to come. He is probably too busy with that girl anyway, she thinks. She doesn't realize she is scowling.

"What's the matter, Angel?" Grandpa wants to know, watching her face.

"Oh, it's just . . ." she hesitates, "so hot, that's all. And Dad should be here by now."

"They'll be along." Grandpa takes time to smile at her. "Probably be here before my lawn service, the rate we're going."

As it happens, everyone arrives at once. Tom Ferris rides into the driveway on his father's little green tractor mower just ahead of the familiar gray Buick with Angela's father at the wheel. Brian rolls down the window to shout some greeting to Tom, as if they are long-lost companions. Angela is resentful that she can't go out right away to say hello, because if she does, Brian will wonder why she isn't speaking to Tom. She klunks down spoons and forks as she sets the table, thinking how complicated her life seems and yet how dull—full of small snags and long empty stretches, like now. Do other people feel this way? she wonders, and wishes briefly to be Tessa, or at least someone other than Angela.

The rain Gram has been waiting for begins in splatters, with far-off thunder. "I'd better turn off this oven," Gram says. She is wary of electrical storms.

"Don't worry, Gram, it isn't bad." The words have barely cleared Angela's lips when there is a single ear-splitting crack overhead and the sky seems to lose control, sending rain straight downward like water from a tap. The kitchen screen flies open, and in comes everyone who was outside: Grandpa, Dad with his arm around his wife's damp shoulders, Brian, and behind Brian, Tom Ferris. The boys pause to drip on the mat just inside the door. A panic of sorts seizes Angela. She thinks she would rather be struck by a bolt from this storm than be civil to Tom.

And whatever Brian chooses to say, it will be awkward.

She flashes her father a quick smile. "Hi, Dad," she says, and thinks fast. "I have to run in and see if GrandMin's all right. I thought I heard her bell." This is a small lie; Min's bell has not rung for days.

The kitchen is crowded and noisy. "Can we give you some supper, Tom?" Gram is saying. In the confusion it is easy for Angela to slip quickly through the dining room and short hallway to GrandMin. No one will come to get her, at least for a while, busy as they'll be with talking. Maybe by then she'll have thought of another way to avoid Tom.

Min's room is almost dark; rain thrums outside the window with a steady, mechanical sound. Angela is careful to make little noise of her own; Min is napping, she thinks, undisturbed by the thunder. Angela stands at the window, as distant from the bed as she can get, staring between the blind's narrow slats into the blur of water trapped in the tiny openings of the screen. She feels invisible.

"Who are you?" The whisper is so unexpected that Angela's knees are shaky as she turns.

"It's just me, GrandMin. Angela." She struggles to adjust her eyes so that she can see her great-grandmother's face. "Does the storm bother you?"

Min seems not to have heard. "Angela?" she repeats, slowly, as if she is a child mouthing a brand-new word. Her breathing is very slow. "You look familiar," she says at last.

Angela sighs. "I should," she says. "You've seen me every day for weeks now, not to mention all those years since I was a baby."

Min takes a big breath; Angela waits for her to say something more. Outside, the wind has risen, and it slams the rain against the house. Angela steps cautiously toward the bed for the sake of hearing GrandMin better, but there is nothing to hear. Angela would think that Min has drifted off to sleep now, but how can she be sleeping with her eyes so wide?

"GrandMin?" whispers Angela to the silence on the bed. "GrandMin?" She stretches one hand to touch the old woman's shoulder, to touch her and make her breathe.

At that moment the door swings wide and Brian comes into the room. "Hey, Buff," he says, "you didn't even say hello to me."

Angela straightens up, trembling. For once all her feelings are plain in her face. Brian glances from her to the staring figure on the bed.

"Hey," he says again, in a different tone, and

reaches behind his back to flip on the overhead light. GrandMin's eyes do not blink.

Angela swallows, pushing down the thing inside that threatens to overwhelm her. "Do you think she's . . ." The word will not come.

Brian's face is blank with wonder. "Come on," he says. He turns off the light and reaches for his sister's hand, as though they are little again. "We'll go get Gram."

———

First there was Harry, and then Winthrop and Ben and Firman Junior, and next Walter. Lucy's babies came with a regularity that amused most of Jericho and dismayed her family, especially Min, who was childless and therefore expected to help out. It was more charity toward poor beleaguered Blossom Clark than affection for her sister that moved her, although she did admit to falling in love with each of Lucy's little boys in turn.

For Min no babies came, much as she wanted them, expected them, prayed for them. She tried every tonic advertised, every foolish trick the old women whispered about. Leo wanted a child, too, she could tell, but he never talked of it. After they had been married six years with nothing to show for it, as Lucy often said, Leo brought Min a puppy. She named it Red and made it her baby.

Red slept in the house in a pasteboard box cut to look like a real bed, ate from a china bowl that was only a little bit cracked, and learned to do tricks. Min was so taken with the little dog that Leo next brought her a kitten, then two baby ducks, and after that a kid, a tiny goat with an appetite for destruction.

"Enough!" Min pronounced, but the back lot was already so exciting that Lucy's older boys begged to visit Min and Grandpa every day. Even Will's children came from time to time.

After she had given up on babies, resigned herself to life as Auntie Min, a grown woman with no girlishness left in her body, that was when she noticed the signs and knew she was in the family way. It was hard from the beginning—for Lucy, too, who had to learn to make do without her. Toward the end of her time, the doctor ordered Min off her feet. From the daybed in the kitchen, she gave her father step-by-step instructions for making supper. She darned every sock in the house, Leo's and Pa's and her own, and stitched up a layette that Leo said would do a Rockefeller proud. She read the New Liberty paper through so many times every week that she could recite by heart the wrongdoings of those rascals in Europe.

And then when it was time, the baby wouldn't come. Doctor Shindler came and went half a dozen times. Old Mrs. Allison, who tended all the women in Jericho, came and stayed. Leo was banished to the barn, to the fields, anywhere. Sam Walters wouldn't budge from his chair by the kitchen stove, no matter how much coming and going there was.

"She's my baby," he said. The dog had to stay chained in the yard.

Min couldn't think straight; she lost track of time there in Pa's bedroom just off the kitchen. It was summer, and one storm after another rolled over the cemetery hill and on into town. Sometimes she thought she could feel the thunder in her bones, the fire of the lightning on her skin. But the heat was only summer wrapping itself around her when the windows were closed against the rain.

Sometimes in her long, troubled labor Min dreamed. She dreamed of Sammy, she dreamed of Delia, and she dreamed at last of her mother. Molly Walters stood on a hillside in a flurry of snow, waving her apron and shouting with no words, trying to call out something of great importance, though no one could tell what it was.

Min came awake to the sounds of rain and Leo's shouting in the kitchen.

"Do something, Shindler! Do something! I don't want to her to die! I can't bear to lose her!"

At the same time Mrs. Allison's voice was urging her. "Finally, Arminda! Be strong now. Now! *Now!*"

She thought the lightning must have struck her, but it was the baby. All at once the baby was there. Leo ranted so in the kitchen and made so much noise that he missed his wife's weak shout and the infant's first mewling cry.

"A girl baby," Mrs. Allison announced, and held the glistening little creature aloft for Min's bleary-eyed inspection.

"Ahhh." Min was too tired to examine her accomplishment. In her head she searched and found the names she had stored away so that she could whisper the right one: "Katherine. Little Katy." She filled up with silent exultation.

"Leo!" Mrs. Allison summoned the father with such an imperious screech that the baby squirmed. "Dr. Shindler!"

"Please don't let her die, Shindler," Leo was still saying as the two men crowded through the door.

Min found enough energy to smile up at them. Dear, foolish Leo. Of course she wasn't going to die. She was a mother with a child to look after. She felt that she would live forever.

EPILOGUE

THE FUNERAL IS OVER now, and GrandMin is safe with her family. It seems funny, Angela thinks, to have her lying up in the cemetery beside her long-dead husband instead of here at Gram's, in the front bedroom. Angela's father keeps rubbing the back of her mother's neck. "It was like taking her home," Carol says. "Remember? She used to play up there." Grandpa nods; he is wearing a suit for only the second time within Angela's memory.

Angela worries that Gram will fall apart now, but she doesn't. The neighbors have brought cakes and casseroles and generous hugs, all sustaining things. Angela takes the most pleasure in the flowers that have been sent to Gram. They are beautiful in ways that she realizes she doesn't understand; they seem to protect her imagination from the ugly things that it wants to create. Tessa says they are the most spectacular flowers she has ever seen.

Angela is sure beyond a doubt that her parents love her, because they knew without being told what she would need to get her through these last few days. One call home to Tessa's mother, one trip to the bus station in New Liberty, and there was Tessa. She has left her fake fingernails at home in honor of the death in the family, and most of the time she remembers not to squeal when she talks. Hearing her steady breathing at night from the sleeping bag beside the couch is a great comfort.

Tessa insists that this trip is as good as a vacation. Angela thinks she will change her mind when she notices the absence of pizza places and video rentals in Gatesville, but maybe by then they can both go home. For the time being, she is happy that Tessa is happy. She doesn't even mind that Tessa watches Brian like a hungry owl after a mouse. It is a measure of her friend's generosity, Angela thinks, that she expresses such interest in the tale of Tom Ferris. Angela is still embarrassed, almost repulsed, to think of him, but Tessa insists she must change her attitude.

"It was an experience, Ange. You have to have those before you can find someone who's worth it, you know?"

Angela doesn't know, but she is glad to have Tessa here to talk about it. They are sitting cross-legged on the floor, drinking pop and looking through the old pictures that Gram has still not had a chance to finish labeling.

"Mostly question marks," observes Tessa, turning them over one by one.

"Umm," agrees Angela. She has found the photograph that Gram thinks is Aunt Lucy, thrown back in with all the others.

"Angela!" Tessa's voice is suddenly urgent. "Did you see this? Look at this!"

Angela glances at the picture in Tessa's hand. A young woman's face, vaguely familiar, stares up at her. The brows are straight, the eyes are clear, the expression determined. Whoever it is wears a wrinkled ribbon around her high collar.

"Ange, when you're older, you'll look exactly like this. I mean, you would if you wore these clothes and did weird stuff with your hair."

"Oh, no way," says Angela for Tessa's benefit, but she reaches for the picture with a thudding heart. She recognizes this face. It is the one she has been hoping to discover when she looks in the mirror.

"Who is it?" Tessa demands.

Angela looks at the back of the photo. At first she thinks this picture will be as much a mystery as the others. And then she sees, in the lightest of pencil, in an awkward, old-fashioned hand: *My dearest Arminda.*

For that first speechless moment she feels a sense of connection so strong and so unsettling that she thinks she cannot bear it.

"So do you know who it is?" Tessa reaches for the picture. "Come on, I want to know."

But Angela is holding the old portrait so tightly that her fingertips are turning from pink to white. "It's her," she says slowly. "My great-grandmother."

"No!" Tessa bends in amazement over the photo, then leans back to consider her friend's face.

"Oh, Tessa," Angela says, and she doesn't know whether she will laugh or cry. "It's GrandMin. Just imagine!"